# BOOM!

A play with music

by
Darren Rapier

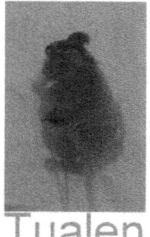

Tualen

Tualen Press
PO Box 239
Sidcup
DA16 0DP
info@spannerintheworks.org.uk


First Published 2008

© Darren Rapier 2008
www.darrenrapier.co.uk

ISBN 978-0-9556798-2-7

For a copy of the original songs email
info@darrenrapier.co.uk

For performance rights of this play please contact:

Andrew Mann Ltd.,
1 Old Compton Street,
London, W1D 5JA
Tel: 020 7734 4751
Fax: 020 7287 9264
info@andrewmann.co.uk

**BOOM!** was first presented by Bexley Council as part of the Danson Millennium Festival on the 29th June 2000. The production was **directed by Nick Pilton**, with **Musical Direction by Cate Gibbs** and had the following cast:

Mother Bomullock - Carole Moulton
Mr. Bomullock – David Munns
Katherine Bomullock – Lynne Jones
Mr. Greenbag – Matt Clowry
Children – Emerald Jones, Deborah Knox-Hewson, Georgina
Harris, Rebecca Pearce, Perry Millward.
Mistress – Debbie Stickland
Tilly – Laura Latcham
Lucy – Ashlie Edwards
Mr. Leech – Steve Smith
Mr. Hurst – Jonathan Rooks
Anne Hurst – Kerrie Weller
Agnes Hurst – Sarah Thomas
Alice Hurst – Victoria Barry
Dot – Janet Knox -Hewson
Bertie – Mark Pike
Mr. Arden - David Munns
Lady Knotchel – Judie Richardson
Mary – Lauren Chance
Shanks – Vanessa Harris
Slick Joe – Dave Millwood
Charlie – Gary Holloway
The Kid – Mark Keevil
Grace – Michael Girton
The Manor House Ghost – Mark Pike
Howard – Lorne Thomson
Jane – Aimee Gladding
Edd – Matt Clowry
Iris – Emma Stewart
Bea – Sally Brooks
Ginny – Claire Potter
Ruth – Lisa Millwood
Isobel – Katy Latcham
Sarah – Mandy Bridges
Mr. Dray – David Munns
Gypsy/ Teller - Debbie Stickland
Iron Lady –Katy Johnson
Doreen – Jill Bavington Pearce
Lady Woolward – Katy Latcham
Lady Tulchan – Claire Potter
Mr. Tench – Mark Pike
Trusty – Judie Richardson
Gloria Duvall – Jill Bavington Pearce

## Characters

**Mother Bomullock**
**Mr. Bomullock** – her son
**Katherine Bomullock** – her daughter-in-law
**Mr. Greenbag** – agent for the estate
**Children** – from local children's home
**Mistress** – their teacher
**Tilly** – Bomullock's neighbour, works at Vickers
**Lucy** – her sister
**Mr. Leech** – window salesperson
**Mr. Hurst** – an old farmer
**Anne Hurst** – his eldest daughter
**Agnes Hurst** – his middle daughter
**Alice Hurst** – his youngest daughter
**Dot** – a secretary at a signwriters
**Bertie** – a signwriter
**Mr. Arden** - a garage owner
**Lady Knotchel** – an aristocrat
**Mary** – her servant
**Shanks** – a local villain
**Slick Joe** – his deputy
**Charlie** – gang member
**The kid** – gang member
**Flo** – gang member
**Grace** – gang member
**The Manor House Ghost** – a ghostly figure

**Howard** – Tilly's brother
**Jane** – Edd's servant
**Edd** – a London builder
**Iris** – a nurse at Queen Mary's Hospital
**Bea** – a worker at Vickers
**May** – a worker at Vickers
**Ginny** – a worker at Vickers
**Ruth** – a worker at the laundry
**Isobel** – a worker at the laundry
**Sarah** – the foreman at the laundry
**Mr. Dray** – the manager of the laundry
**Gypsy** – a local settled traveller
**Teller** - her friend
**Gypsy Children** – other local travellers
**Iron Lady** – a lady who demonstrates irons
**Doreen** – a television saleswoman
**Lady Woolward** – friend of Lady Knotchel's
**Lady Tulchan** – friend of Lady Knotchel's
**Mr. Tench** – a local builder
**Trusty** – Gloria Duvall's agent
**Reporters** – from local and national papers
**Gloria Duvall** – a singing star

# BOOM!
## By Darren Rapier

*The staging suggests a green outdoor feel, perhaps even
with trees in the background. As the play progresses
each scene adds a man-made colour or texture. We
move from exterior to interior, until (by the end) the
stage is dressed in shades of grey – representing the
shift from country to suburb.*

### Boom

In nineteen-fourteen,
The South East was green,
The average scene,
Was one of farms.

Along came the war,
Like the previous Boer,
Made arms production soar,
And the guns went Boom!

Boom, boom, boom,
Boom, boom, boom,
Boom, the guns went boom!

Boom, boom, boom,
Boom, boom, boom,
Boom, boom, boom, boom, Boom!

Around twenty-nine,
Things seemed to be fine,
The healing of time,
Calmed stormy tides.

But over the sea,
The economy,
Went very shaky,
And the banks went Boom!

Boom, boom, boom,
Boom, boom, boom,
Boom, the banks went boom!

Boom, boom, boom,
Boom, boom, boom,

Boom, boom, boom, boom, Boom!

Yet the South-East was saved,
By the plans of the day,
To build anyway,
As London spread.
Schemes started to loom,
They began to assume,
That we had the room,
So the houses went Boom!

Boom, boom, boom,
Boom, boom, boom,
Boom, the houses went boom!

Boom, boom, boom,
Boom, boom, boom,
Boom, boom, boom, boom, BOOM!

### **SCENE ONE:   Site of a New House - January 1936**


*MOTHER BOMULLOCK, MR. BOMULLOCK and
KATHERINE are being shown around by MR.
GREENBAG.*

GREENBAG:      …And if you step in here, you will find the
bathroom:  Hot and cold running water, inside
toilet – of course – and a fixed bath.

MOTHER BOMULLOCK: What's wrong with a tub?

GREENBAG:      Nothing, nothing wrong with a tub.   But this
house has room for all the 'modern
conveniences'.

*A gaggle of CHILDREN from the Children's home at
the Hollies walk down the street, following their
MISTRESS..*

M BOMULLOCK:   *(Disdainfully)*   What are those?

GREENBAG:      Those?   They're children Mrs. Bomullock.

M BOMULLOCK:   I can see that.   But why are they here, in
our street?

*One of the CHILDREN sticks their tongue out at
MOTHER BOMULLOCK.*

GREENBAG:      Oh, they're from the children's home at the
Hollies.   As I was saying, these houses are
built for today's modern lifestyle.   Some even
have a garage for a car.   There's electricity
throughout, for any of the new labour saving
devices:   we wouldn't want the young Mrs.
Bomullock here spoiling her lovely hands, on
all that scrubbing of clothes.

M. BOMULLOCK: Electricity eh?

GREENBAG:      Yes.   Electricity will revolutionise our lives,
lighting, cooking, heating – all at the flick of a

switch. The day'll come when we'll be lost without it.

BOMULLOCK: What happens when it runs out?

GREENBAG: How do you mean?

BOMULLOCK: What happens when all the electricity runs out? When it's all used up? What'll we do then, go back to coal?

GREENBAG: It won't 'run out'.

BOMULLOCK: That's what they said about whale oil.

KATHERINE: It's not like a fuel.

BOMULLOCK: Was I talking to you? Was I?

GREENBAG: Besides, the Blackwall cable's reinforced supplies to the area, there's no chance of a failure.

M. BOMULLOCK: What's wrong with gas lighting?

GREENBAG: No, no, there's no facility for gas lighting.

M. BOMULLOCK: Well that doesn't seem very forward thinking in my book.

GREENBAG: People don't want gas any more. Ideal Homesteads are exactly that: Ideal. These houses represent the best of what's new and fresh. They know the working classes won't fill their bathrooms with coal...

*He looks at MOTHER BOMULLOCK.*

GREENBAG: They say 'give people bathrooms and inside toilets', 'give them the chance to use the energy of the future' and most importantly make it affordable. I tell you Sub-urbanisation is here to stay. You're only thirty-five minutes by train or car into the centre of London and here you've got the countryside at your doorstep.

*TILLY and her young sister LUCY cycle in.*

TILLY: Are you moving in?

M. BOMULLOCK: How dare you cycle into our bathroom.

TILLY: It's not quite a bathroom yet is it? Just a square in a muddy field, same as ours.

LUCY: Me and Tills are going to have our own bedroom.

M BOMULLOCK: Are you from the children's home?

TILLY: No, we're from East Ham.

M BOMULLOCK: (*Under her breath*) Even worse.

TILLY: Any progress Mr. Greenbag?

GREENBAG: As you can see, the whole of West Wood's been cleared, in fact there's only six plots left in this road.

TILLY: I see all the houses are occupied in Belle Grove.

GREENBAG: Yes, it doesn't take long.

M. BOMULLOCK: Do you mind?

TILLY: Oh, sorry. The name's Tilly and this is Lucy; we'll be neighbours.

BOMULLOCK: How can you afford a house?

TILLY: You can afford anything at the right price. Besides, my dad's been left some money.

*Beat.*

LUCY: We've been down to the Bexley Heath clock tower, for the proclamation.

TILLY: There were hundreds of people there - waiting for the announcement - 'Corse we'd all heard it on the wireless, but it's not the same is it?

BOMULLOCK: One King's much the same as another.

TILLY: It's exciting though isn't it? We'll be able to have a street party for the coronation - once there's a street to have it in.

M BOMULLOCK: I don't like street parties, all and sundry rubbing elbows at the same table, showing off their cutlery and china, like some department at Jones and Higgins.

TILLY: Where abouts are you from?

KATHERINE: Southwark.

M. BOMULLOCK: Don't encourage her.

BOMULLOCK: (*To Greenbag*) What about those houses down at Barne Hurst? You can choose how you want the rooms laid out.

TILLY: (*To Katherine*) I love it here. The air's so clear, it feels like someone's polished the inside of your eyes.

GREENBAG: Why do you want the bother of designing the interior layout of your house? Let a professional worry about that.

TILLY: We're on our way back to the ferry, it don't take long. Does it Luce?

BOMULLOCK: We'll think about it.

GREENBAG: Don't think on it too long, the house buying season's only a few months away.

M. BOMULLOCK: Think of the price son.

GREENBAG: Your mother's right, sir. There's houses up the road at Bexley Heights starting at £895, some of them are knocking two thousand. Like I said, these are an ideal family home:

spare bedroom for the children, you'll be laughing.  Confidentially, the way prices are going in this area, I'd sign up as soon as I could.

*LEECH has glided into the gathering, unnoticed.*

LEECH:          I suppose you'll be having the standard windows?

LUCY:           Look Tilly it's that man again.

BOMULLOCK: What do you mean standard?

GREENBAG:   This is private property.

LEECH:          Public Road.

M. BOMULLOCK: Will everybody please get out of our bathroom!

GREENBAG:   The windows are perfectly adequate for these houses…

LEECH:          Over the main road they've got a bit more class, fitted Critall to start with.  Here take my card.

BOMULLOCK: What's this?

GREENBAG:   It's a blooming liberty, that's what it is.

LEECH:          Ideal Homesteads import all their stuff: Windows from Czechoslovakia, bricks from Belgium, keeps the price down you see...

GREENBAG:   I'll call the Coppers.

*LEECH looks at him and starts to skulk off..*

LEECH:          (*Leaving*) Don't loose that card now, it'll keep your heating bill down and add to the price of your property.

GREENBAG:   I do apologise, these Critall window salesmen won't leave you alone.

- 11 -

TILLY: My dad says they'll still move in the heat and cold, same as a wooden window. More chance of cracking the glass he reckons.

KATHERINE: Is he a carpenter?

LUCY: Boiler maker.

TILLY: Knows a lot about metal. Can't find the work now mind.

KATHERINE: Is that why you're moving here?

TILLY: He's bought a fruit shop over near Pen Hill, no-one needs boiler makers any more.

LUCY: I'm going to help him in the shop on Saturdays.

GREENBAG: What sort of work do you do Mr. Bomullock?

BOMULLOCK: None of your business.

*GREENBAG smiles nervously.*

BOMULLOCK: All right, we'll take it. At the price, it's the best we ain't seen. Still seems a lot of tush for a pile of bricks, mind.

TILLY: Then we will be neighbours!

GREENBAG: Thank heaven's for the building societies eh?

BOMULLOCK: Cash.

GREENBAG: Oh, er... Right, well if you'd like to come back to my office we can sort out the paper work.

M. BOMULLOCK: How long will it take?

GREENBAG: Oh, about a month.

M. BOMULLOCK: I mean to finish the house.

GREENBAG:     About a month.   This is the last house in this
              terrace and we're working on a three week
              construction period, from start to finish.

BOMULLOCK:  How can you get them up so quick?

GREENBAG:     A thirsty workforce.   There are some benefits
              on the coat tails of a depression.

TILLY:        So we can move in by February?

GREENBAG:     I can't see a problem there.   By then every
              country lane and dirt track you see will be a
              smart new street.

### Boom (Reprise)

(Whispered):

              Boom, boom, boom,
              Boom, boom, boom,
              Boom, boom, boom, boom, boom!

              Boom, boom, boom,
              Boom, boom, boom,
              Boom, boom, boom, boom, Boom!

## SCENE TWO: A Frost-baked field on Mr. Hurst's Farm - January 1936

*HURST stumbles his way across the field with his three daughters.*

ANNE: My feet are like blocks of ice

AGNES: Slow down pa, you're not following the plough horse now.

ALICE: (*To Hurst*) Watch your step, the ground's as hard as rock.

ANNE: I can't see why we need to come all the way out here?

HURST: You'll see soon enough.

AGNES: My shoes are completely ruined.

HURST: You shouldn't wear slippers out in the fields, any farmer knows that.

AGNES: Well I'm not a farmer, am I? Anyway they're not slippers, they are the height of fashion in London.

HURST: Here we are.

ANNE: Where?

HURST: Smell that.

AGNES: Cow shit?

HURST: Countryside. That's what you can smell. Remember the smell girls, it'll soon be washed out.

AGNES: I hope so, this dress cost an absolute fortune. Now it reeks like a badger's breakfast.

ALICE: So why did you bring us up here Pa?

| | |
|---|---|
| HURST: | The passing of the King sets your mind to work, sets you off thinking about your own life. |
| ALICE: | You've got years to go yet. |
| HURST: | Years start to tumble into decades, 'fore you know it life's snuck past you. |
| ANNE: | Couldn't we have talked about this at the house? |
| AGNES: | In front of a nice fire? |
| HURST: | We're guided by nature , don't you forget it. You can't ignore it; we can flatten it, burn it, build over it, but it's always here.  And slowly, slowly it'll take back into nature what came from nature.  The cracks in the pavements spawn green shoots, the hard red brick is softened by the velvet moss.  Nothing we can do can stop it. |
| AGNES: | You're not suggesting we should live out here? We'd freeze to death. |
| ALICE: | Agnes. |
| HURST: | I'm saying, trying to brush nature aside is a folly.  We need it, we need to understand it: Use it, work with it.  These fields will be here long after me. |
| ALICE: | Not at the rate they're building, at the moment. |
| HURST: | Exactly my girl, exactly.  And it's up to us to make sure we never lose sight of the land. That's why I want a pledge from each of you. |
| ANNE: | What sort of a pledge? |
| HURST: | I'm getting too old to manage the farm, you get forgetful, I can hear the labourers sniggering at me behind my back. |
| ALICE: | That's not true. |

| | |
|---|---|
| HURST: | True or no, there's too much to think on for an old man. |
| AGNES: | Well I'm already doing as much as I can, Alice will have to help you organise things, she doesn't have a job. |
| HURST: | Alice is the only one of you who could step into the running of a farm, who actually knows what goes on. |
| ANNE: | That's unfair. I run a whole department at Hide's, have you any idea how much organisation that takes? |
| ALICE: | I think pa is merely saying that we have to appreciate there are different priorities to farm work. |
| HURST: | It's no use thinking it's the same as any other business, you've got to understand the land. |
| AGNES: | That's all very well, but what's the point of telling us? We're never going to have farms of our own. |
| HURST: | That is why you're here. I don't want to leave the farm to someone who don't know his oats from his elbow. |
| AGNES: | So you're expecting us to marry farmers now? |
| HURST: | I'm expecting you to learn how to farm, in return for a third of the land. And that goes for all of you. If you can prove to me that you're capable of running a small farm, by the Spring, it's yours. |
| ANNE: | You're giving us the farm? |
| ALICE: | Then what will you do? |
| HURST: | I have no need of money, now your mother's gone, what's there to do? I'll keep the farm house of course, but I'll not own a clump of earth. |

ALICE:      Why do you want to give us the farm now?

HURST:      Because, while there's a drop of breath still in me, I have influence.  There's a shortage of good men my dears and a lady's more attractive if she's got property.  They'll be swarming like flies around a honey pot.  You don't want to be taken in by some London property developer, keen on paving over the whole place - like at Pelham.

AGNES:      So you are choosing us husbands?

HURST:      Not at all.  I'm ensuring the future of the farm, that's why I need your pledge.

ANNE:       Of what?

HURST:      That , if I give you a share in the farm, you won't ever consider selling it for development.

AGNES:      Then it's not ours?

HURST:      It's up to you what to grow, how best to manage it.

ANNE:       So, legally we will own one third of the farm each?

HURST:      Three separate farms technically, how you work it out together is up to you.  All I ask is to be allowed to stay at the farm house, free of charge.

AGNES:      And we are free to marry whomsoever we wish?

HURST:      Of course.

ANNE:       But the land will be ours, by deed?

HURST:      I've already spoken to the solicitor, all we need do is set a date.  But remember, you must show me you are capable of running your own plot, independently of any help from your sisters.

AGNES:      For three months?

HURST:      Forever, once it's in your possession.

ANNE:      Will we be legally bound to keep the whole area as farmland?

HURST:      Apparently it's too restrictive, in case you wanted to build another farm house or something. Your word is good enough for me.

AGNES:      Our pledge?

HURST:      Once you get used to tending the land you won't want to go back to shop work. Nature has her own rewards.

ANNE:      I'm sure she does.

ALICE:      But, the climate is against small farms, like ours, if we split it further…

ANNE:      Very well, I'll do it.

ALICE:      Run a farm?

ANNE:      Yes, it's just a matter of organising things. I expect I'll be quite good. I have, deep down, always had a fondness for agriculture.

HURST:      That's my girl, we won't turn our fields over to these hop pickers' sons.

ANNE:      I shall hand in my notice on Monday.

ALICE:      Is that wise?

AGNES:      Me too.

ALICE:      I thought you hated farming?

AGNES:      I have always hankered after an outdoor life.

HURST:      It's in your blood girl.

AGNES:          Yes, I suppose it is.  You know, I can't wait
                to start reaping in the harvest with my stickle.

ALICE:          That's sickle.

AGNES:          Besides, land of your own gives you a certain
                incentive.

HURST:          Then I have your word, the farm will never be
                sold for development?

AGNES/ANNE: Yes.

HURST:          Good.  And what about you Alice?  You have
                helped me these last years more than anyone, I
                have no doubt you will make a sterling farmer.

        *Beat.*

ALICE:          How can I make such a pledge?

HURST:          How do you mean?

ALICE:          Look around you.  We are hemmed in by
                building.  The soil is rough, the autumn frost
                killed our apple crop last year, no one's eating
                potatoes.  The pickers won't want to come
                here, they'll go further out into Kent.  And,
                when their families have all got houses on the
                old farms, they won't even do that.

HURST:          What are you trying to say?

ALICE:          Who knows what the future has in store for us?
                I can only pledge to keep the farm going as
                long as possible.

HURST:          As long as possible?  As long as possible!?
                And how long is that?

ALICE:          I don't know.  If you feel unable to cope
                perhaps the time is now.

HURST:          What!!

ANNE:           Before he gives it to us?

ALICE:      There's no need to give it to us, you could get a good price now, retire. All the work you've put in over the years, well... it could give you the chance to enjoy the rest of your life.

HURST:      This is my life! And you want to discard it, like a cracked jug?

ALICE:      I didn't say that. I simply said I couldn't make a pledge.

AGNES:      Then perhaps you don't deserve a chance to own it.

ALICE:      The only harvest you're looking forward to is the one where you can bail up your bank notes.

HURST:      Don't speak to your sister like that.

ALICE:      Well look at them, where have they been these last few years?

ANNE:       We wanted to help more, but you insisted on doing everything.

AGNES:      Probably thought that he'd leave you the whole farm.

ALICE:      I did not.

HURST:      Was that your plan?

ALICE:      What plan?

HURST:      To get the farm, sell it off for development after I was gone?

ALICE:      No.

AGNES:      She hates farming.

ANNE:       We've never had the chance to show how much we love working the land.

AGNES:      Alice always tries to make it look as if we're not interested.

| | |
|---|---|
| HURST: | Alright, alright, that's enough?  Now, Alice, do you want a third of the farm? |
| ALICE: | It's not up to me to ask... |
| HURST: | Then will you make a pledge to me, that you will keep the land for agricultural use? |
| ALICE: | I'm not lying to you, simply for my own gain. |
| HURST: | Then you will not make a pledge? |
| ALICE: | How can I? |
| HURST: | Of the three of you I had thought you to be true, to live by my principals, but now I see you are merely a hollow shell – eaten away inside by greed. |
| ALICE: | I ask nothing of you. |
| HURST: | Nothing will come of nothing.  This night has opened my eyes, the frost has sharpened my vision.  I will not leave land to someone who, before it is even within her grip, sees profit in it's sale. |
| ALICE: | I don't want it. |
| HURST: | And you shall not have it!  I'll go to see the solicitors tomorrow and, by the turn of the Sun, you will have no more part in this land than any surveyor's level. |
| ALICE: | I... |
| HURST: | Do not speak.  My senses are closed to you. |

*HURST exits, followed by a smug ANNE and AGNES.*

## **Brick by Brick**

Brick by brick,
Brick by brick,
Brick by brick *(Repeat under as...)*

One dark night,
The city crept out,
From under the gas lights,
And snuck into the country.

No one noticed,
As the march of clay,
Slipped over the green grass,
And set rock hard on the way.

When morning cracked open,
To their surprise,
A man made brickscape,
Stretched out before their eyes.

Lanes and dirt tracks,
Spawned avenues of tar,
And the carts and horses yielded,
To the shining armour of the car.

Where once stood trees,
Razor stones cut the knuckles of their sight,
And the pollen soaked breeze,
Was caught and drowned in the cables of
electrolyte.

So when did it?
Why did it?
How did it?

Brick by brick,
Brick by brick,
Brick by brick....

### SCENE THREE:   The forecourt of a Bexleyheath Car Showroom - February 1936

*BERTIE and DOT wait for the return of MR. ARDEN, the garage owner.   The CHILDREN are running around.*

BERTIE:        Oi, get off that car!

CHILD:         Ain't yours

BERTIE:        So, show some respect.

CHILD:         Who for, the cat's mother?

*Thinking this is hilarious the CHILDREN fall about giggling.*

BERTIE:        I'll give you a clip round the ear in a minute.

DOT:           Oh, just ignore them.

CHILD:         You'll have to catch us first.

*The CHILD starts to run off, but bumps into the MISTRESS.   Terror fills them.*

MISTRESS:      If you cannot be trusted to behave – which it appears you can't – then perhaps it is best I do not take you out?   I think you should all apologise to this man, for being so rude.

CHILDREN:      (*Grudgingly*)   Sorry.

MISTRESS:      And next time I go into a shop I expect to find you all outside, waiting attentively.

CHILDREN:      Yes Miss, sorry Miss.

MISTRESS:      You may not have parents, but you can still have manners.

*The CHILDREN silently file out, followed by the MISTRESS.*

DOT: I don't know why you had to come along, I only need the details for the sign board.

BERTIE: Merely to ensure Mr. Arden's pleased with the sign.

DOT: He'll not give you a car, you know.

BERTIE: I'm not asking him to give me a car.

DOT: But you wouldn't say no, if he did?

BERTIE: Who would? Anyway, he wouldn't miss one would he? We could sign write the doors for him, advertise his garage all round Bexley.

DOT: If you could drive.

BERTIE: Oh it won't be long now, got my test date booked for the summer.

DOT: And a space in the paper?

BERTIE: How do you mean?

DOT: For when you get your first speeding fine?

BERTIE: My dad's been teaching me, in the old Oxford.

DOT: He's braver than I thought.

*A car is heard driving away.*

ARDEN: (*Off*) Cheery bye sir, happy driving.

*ARDEN enters.*

BERTIE: Another satisfied customer Mr. Arden?

ARDEN: Oh, hello Bertie. I wasn't expecting you here again today.

BERTIE: I'm here on business today Mr. Arden, making sure your new sign is exactly as you want it.

ARDEN: Oh, oh that's er... smashing. What happened to those kids?

|          | Have to watch the little buggers, had someone break in and steal two lamps the other day. |
| BERTIE:  | Really? |
| DOT:     | It's all these Londoners moving in, only used to happen at hop picking time before. |
| ARDEN:   | Yes, that's true.  I see another estate's opened in Bexley Heath this week. |
| BERTIE:  | That's 'Bexleyheath' Mr. Arden, all one word. Remember, sounds more like 'Blackheath', attracts the right people. |
| DOT:     | Talking of spelling:  I'd just like to check on the spelling and layout for your new sign, before the boys start painting it up for you. |
| ARDEN:   | I see. |
| DOT:     | Now... |
| BERTIE:  | Are you keeping busy Mr. Arden? |
| ARDEN:   | Yes, yes I suppose I am.  The petrol tax isn't helping, but then cars are cheaper so it keeps the punters happy. |
| BERTIE:  | But you could always sell more? |
| ARDEN:   | Erm, not really... I haven't got the space. |
| BERTIE:  | You need a slogan. |
| ARDEN:   | A slogan? |
| BERTIE:  | Oh yes, everyone's got one now - something catchy, inspiring, something that makes people think: 'Wow I need that'.  Something like: 'Glitto Kills Grease'. |
| DOT:     | Glitto Kills Grease? |
| ARDEN:   | Why would I want a sign that says Glitto Kills Grease?  I don't even sell Glitto. |

BERTIE:     No, that was just an example.

DOT:        What of, your stupidity?

BERTIE:     An example of a slogan that works.

ARDEN:      So you're saying I should stock Glitto?

BERTIE:     Look, forget Glitto.   You need something else.

DOT:        There is nothing else, if you want to kill grease.

BERTIE:     To sell cars, a slogan to sell cars.

ARDEN:      But I'm selling plenty of cars.

DOT:        So, your sign reads:  Arden's…

BERTIE:     All I'm saying is you need more than just a name and telephone number to impress people these days.

ARDEN:      I think a telephone number is impressive, there's plenty without.

DOT:        I agree, it's a symbol of success.   People know they can simply pick up the phone and get all the information they want down a wire.

BERTIE:     I don't wish to labour the point, but look at the signs we're making for the property developers.   They're bright, vibrant, attractive. What made you chose Whittle's to paint your sign?

ARDEN:      You're up the road.

BERTIE:     But you must admit our slogan works:   'The sign people'.

ARDEN:      I didn't realise that was a slogan.

BERTIE:     And then we hit you with, 'Experts in modern publicity'.

DOT: I'll hit you with something in a minute.

BERTIE: I've jotted a few of my ideas down, here. 'Arden's Garage – Where do you want to go today?' No? OK, 'Arden's Garage – Start me up'.

ARDEN: It doesn't really flow.

BERTIE: 'Visit any sight on the world wide...

ARDEN: Stop there, I think I've got one. 'Arden's Garage – Buy your car here'.

BERTIE: That wasn't quite...

DOT: We charge by the letter.

ARDEN: Oh forget it, I'll have the name and phone number.

*BERTIE sighs.*

DOT: So that's 'Arden's Garage: A-R-D-E-N...

*LADY KNOTCHEL struts in with her maid MARY, she starts speaking straight away, ignoring the fact that DOT is in mid sentence.*

KNOTCHEL: Do you have the new Jaguar?

ARDEN: Erm, no your ladyship, we don't sell Jaguar.

KNOTCHEL: Oh what a blasted nuisance. What do you have?

ARDEN: We sell Morris... and Wolseley.

KNOTCHEL: And what are they like?

ARDEN: The Wolseley 14 deluxe is a lovely car. Admittedly it's thirty-five pounds more than the standard model, but well worth it. It has a sliding head, triplex glass, dual arm screen wipers, chrome headlamps - not the usual black enamel. It's even got chrome front &

- 27 -

rear bumpers - you should really consider bumpers on a car these days, they're so much safer. You've got a centre arm rest in the back, a sun visor, roof net…

KNOTCHEL: I think I get the picture. How much?

ARDEN: Two-hundred and thirty five pounds - still a hundred and fifty short of the SS Jag - and, if I may say so, a better car for a lady to drive.

KNOTCHEL: Is it reliable?

ARDEN: Wolseley Lady Knotchel? Last you forever.

KNOTCHEL: Very well, may I see one?

ARDEN: Certainly your ladyship, please step into my showing room.

*ARDEN and LADY KNOTCHEL exit.*

BERTIE: I thought she had a car?

MARY: She wants something smaller, that she can drive herself.

BERTIE: She's sold the Rolls?

MARY: Oh no, she'll keep that for when she needs chauffeuring.

BERTIE: Two cars, what sort of a family has two cars?

DOT: Oh stop it Bertie, you're only jealous.

BERTIE: What's she going to do with a fourteen horse power car? She'll not drive more than ten miles an hour I'll bet.

DOT: (*To* Mary) And why's she brought you along?

MARY: In case she wants company driving back to Hall Place, we're paying a visit on the Countess.

DOT: You're her housemaid, not her skivvy.

| | |
|---|---|
| MARY: | Oh, I don't mind, it gets me out. |
| DOT: | Well you wouldn't catch me going into service, slavery more like. |
| MARY: | It's not that bad. |
| BERTIE: | I think it's disgraceful these toffs living at our expense. |
| DOT: | Who's living at our expense? |
| BERTIE: | The Countess.   We own Hall Place now, what's she doing swanning about up there? |
| MARY: | It's her home. |
| BERTIE: | But it belongs to us. |
| DOT: | What would you have her do, move into a hutment at East Wickham? |
| BERTIE: | Times have changed, there's no room round here for these posh nobs in their big houses any more.   If this was Russia they'd be out on their ear alright.   It's about time they realised that we ain't all going to be tugging our forelocks at them and doing whatever they say. |
| KNOTCHEL: | You, boy.   Would you run and tell my driver I shan't be needing him to take me to Hall Place, there's a dear. |
| BERTIE: | Yes ma'am, right away ma'am |

*BERTIE scuttles off as MARY and DOT snigger to each other.*

### Brick by Brick (reprise)

Brick by brick,
Brick by brick,
Brick by brick…

## SCENE FOUR:  The Boundary of an Empty Manor House - February 1936

*SHANKS and his gang:  SLICK JOE, CHARLIE, THE KID, along with FLO and GRACE loiter outside the gates.*

SHANKS:        Well, go on then, what are you waiting for?

KID:           I thought I saw a light flickering in the window.

SHANKS:        What window?

KID:           That one.

SHANKS:        Get out of it, the place has been empty for the last four weeks.

CHARLIE:       (*Teasing The Kid*)  Maybe it's the 'Manor House Ghost', wooooah.

JOE:           Soon see if anyone's home.

*He throws a stone, there is a loud crash of glass.*

SHANKS:        Oh, well done, Einstein.   Why don't you go to the police box and call the coppers while you're about it?

JOE:           There's no-one around, builder's won't be back 'til tomorrow.

CHARLIE:       Hey Shanks, shall we smash all the windows?

SHANKS:        Why?

CHARLIE:       Well it's a laugh ain't it?

SHANKS:        For schoolboys, yeah.

CHARLIE:       Joe got to smash one.

SHANKS:        Joe's an idiot.

JOE:           Oi.

| | |
|---|---|
| SHANKS: | Now, are we going to do this or not? |
| FLO: | I'm cold. |
| SHANKS: | Well of course you're cold, it's the middle of February. |
| GRACE: | I wish I lived here. |
| CHARLIE: | Not with that window you wouldn't. |
| GRACE: | No, not now. Before, when it was owned by some toffy-nosed Lord. |
| FLO: | Yeah, we could've been frightfully posh. Given you the old run around: 'Would you bring me up some more Ovaltine Charles?'. |
| GRACE: | 'And some of those lovely Polo biscuits'. |
| SHANKS: | Them nobs wouldn't drink Ovaltine. |
| GRACE: | How would you know? |
| SHANKS: | Any way, where do you think you'd have been in a house like that? Scrubbing the scullery, that's where. |
| GRACE: | I would not. |
| SHANKS: | We wouldn't have been able to set foot in a place like this, that's why we might as well make the most of it now. |
| JOE: | Probably nothing in there worth having anyway. |
| SHANKS: | And how would you know? |
| JOE: | 'Cause if there was, then the builders would have had it away by now. |
| GRACE: | Seems a shame to tear it down, don't it? |
| SHANKS: | Be serious, what use is a manor house round here. Look at the space it takes up. |

- 31 -

## **Autocratic Outrage**

With your silver spoons,
And your plush ball rooms,
On this stolen land,
By your daddy's hand.


You think it gives you authority,
To put down the majority,
When all of us can quite plainly see,
That you're no better than him or me.

It's all wrong,
Stops you getting on,
It's time to refuse,
The birth right blues,
And an undemocratic, systematic, autocratic
outrage.

It's an outrage.

We discovered what's real,
On the battle fields,
Lost our respect,
For the few select.

And we will have the authority,
The backing of the majority,
'Cos all of them can quite plainly see,
That you're no better than him or me.

It's all wrong,
Stops you getting on,
It's time to refuse,
The birth right blues
And an undemocratic, systematic, autocratic
outrage.

It's an outrage!

*MUSIC continues to underscore quietly as…*

KID:        What was that?

CHARLIE:    I didn't hear anything.

FLO:              I heard it.

SHANKS:           Are you going in or what?

KID:              Alright, alright.

JOE:              Come on Kid, the picture starts in half an hour.

KID:              Why do I have to go?

JOE:              'Cause you're the smallest.

KID:              Flo's smaller than me.

FLO:              I'm not going in.

CHARLIE:          She's a female.

GRACE:            What difference does that make?

JOE:              Oh for gawd sake I'll go, gimme the torch.

*They all watch as JOE clambers into the grounds. He switches on the torch.*

JOE:              There, see.   Nothing.

*As he turns the beam of the torch towards the house it catches the ghostly figure of a HOODED MAN with a white face.   JOE drops the torch and runs.*

ALL:              ARRRRRRG!!

*The others all scatter like pigeons.
MUSIC flourishes and stops.*

## SCENE FIVE:   The Gardens of the New Welling Houses - Late March 1936

*In the crisp spring air TILLY hangs out the washing in the garden of their new house, as shouts can be heard from next door.*

BOMULLOCK: (*Off*) ...And where's the crust, how do you expect me to eat something I don't know whether I'm at the beginning or the middle of?

KATHERINE:   (*Off*)  I though for sandwiches...

BOMULLOCK: (*Off*)  What kind of soft idiot do you think they'd take me for at the river, with sandwiches o' this?  'Ah look he can't chew 'is crusts, poor lad'.  Do you want me to be the laughing stock of Erith?  They'll be asking where me kid gloves are.  Can't you get anything right?

KATHERINE:   (*Off*)  It's one loaf of bread.

BOMULLOCK: (*Off*)  You dare call that a loaf of bread?  It's more like something the King'd wash his arse with.

*HOWARD (TILLY's brother) comes out of the house, with LUCY .*

HOWARD:   Are they still at it?

TILLY:   'Fraid so.

LUCY:   Can't hear the wireless in the back room.

HOWARD:   What's it about this time?

TILLY:   Sliced bread.

KATHERINE:   (*Off*)  I thought it would be easier, less wasteful...

BOMULLOCK: (*Off*)  How did I get lumbered with such a lazy cow?  Can't even be bothered to cut bread?

KATHERINE:   (*Off*)  I didn't expect to end up with you

- 34 -

either!

BOMULLOCK: (*Off*) How dare you raise your voice to me!

HOWARD: Sliced bread? Didn't we have some of that?

LUCY: It's that square stuff.

*The bread comes flying out of the window.*

LUCY: That's it.

TILLY: What are you looking so smart for?

HOWARD: I'm off to see the Mr. Alkinson, at Martin's Bank.

TILLY: What for?

HOWARD: See if he wants to make an investment.

BOMULLOCK: (*Off*) You should think yourself lucky you've a roof over your head woman. There's many a man in my position would have left you, had you marked as a bad penny.

TILLY: What sort of an investment?

HOWARD: In a dance hall.

TILLY: Oh you're not still on about that?

HOWARD: Why not?

BOMULLOCK: (*Off*) You're only one step away from the gutter my girl, remember that. This is <u>my</u> house. To think I work my fingers to the bone, to provide for you, and this is how you repay me?

TILLY: Who'd go 'round here?

LUCY: I'd go.

HOWARD: Who wants to sit in a dark room full of strangers, looking up at a flickering screen?

|  | Ballrooms are the future Tilly. Get a couple of good bands in a week... |
|---|---|
| TILLY: | We ain't in London... |
| HOWARD: | All the more reason: Not everyone wants to go up West to have a good time, we've got half the population of London living on our doorstep now. |
| BOMULLOCK: | (*Off*) Do you just buy whatever the shop keeper offers you, is that it? Are you that stupid? |
| TILLY: | Anyway why would he loan you money, you've got no assets. |
| HOWARD: | That's where you're wrong. Dad said he'd put up the house. |
| TILLY: | The house? |
| LUCY: | Told you not to tell her. |
| HOWARD: | For the first time in our lives Till we've actually got something to offer. |
| TILLY: | And you're prepared to risk it all? |
| HOWARD: | Look, I've got to go, I don't wanna be late. |
| TILLY: | Howard? |

*HOWARD exits.*

| BOMULLOCK: | (*Off*) Do you think me mother'd 'ave bought it? No, no 'corse she wouldn't. She used to make us our bread, didn't you mother. What do you do all day? Sit and look at your woman's magazines, with all their fancy ideas eh? |
|---|---|
| TILLY: | Did dad really say he'd put up the house? |

*LUCY nods.*

BOMULLOCK: (*Off*) Is this what fills your head full of

nonsense, is it?  Let's have a look at this. Washing machines, vacuum cleaners, what'll it be next?  Machines to wash the dishes I suppose?

LUCY:  Maybe you'll finally be able to find yourself a fella at Howies dance hall?

*TILLY narrows her eyes at LUCY.*

TILLY:  And where are you off to, not an appointment at the bank as well?

LUCY:  No, mum and dad are taking me to see their friend's monkeys.

BOMULLOCK:  (*Off*)  Well that's what I think o' that!

*The magazine comes flying out of the window, pages strewn all over the garden.*

BOMULLOCK:  (*Off*)  Perhaps now you'll have time to actually do something with your life?  Instead of sitting there, bone idle?

TILLY:  Who?

LUCY:  Mr & Mrs Dewey.

TILLY:  (*Sniggering*)  They don't keep monkeys.

LUCY:  They do too.  They've got an apery.

TILLY:  It's not an apery it's an 'apiary'.  And apiaries are for keeping bees in.

LUCY:  Yuch!  We're going to see bees?

TILLY:  Dad wants to get some, so we can make our own honey.

BOMULLOCK:  (*Off*)  I want fresh bread on the table by tea time, not this American rubbish.  And mark my words woman if there ain't, so help me I don't know what I'll do!

*The door slams shut (off).*

MOTHER:        (*Off*)  Lucy, time to go.

TILLY:        (*Gently*)  Go on, 'buzz off'.

> *LUCY scowls and exits.*
> *KATHERINE timidly steps into the garden, to collect up the debris.*

TILLY:        The birds'll never eat that, unless you break it into smaller pieces.

KATHERINE:    Oh, er... Hello Tilly.

TILLY:        I don't think they care much for those women's magazines either.

> *KATHERINE continues to pick up the bits and pieces.*

TILLY:        Look, mum's made some bread, would you like it?

KATHERINE:    No, I...

TILLY:        They've gone out Kath, they'll not need it today.  Bread man's round in the morning.

KATHERINE:    I've probably got time to make some...

TILLY:        Why bother?  You don't have to do everything he says you know.  Here, let me go and get it.

> *TILLY exits and returns with a loaf of bread, wrapped in a tea towel.*

TILLY:        Howard's had a slice off the end, but if you're cutting it when he gets in he'll be none the wiser.

KATHERINE:    Thanks Tilly.

TILLY:        You should get out more, it's not good for you being stuck in there all the time.  Do you want some fruit to go with that?

KATHERINE:    No, thanks.  How's the job going?

| | |
|---|---|
| TILLY: | At Vickers? Great. They reckon we'll be even busier now Hitler's bumping up the German arsenal. |
| KATHERINE: | Do you think there'll be another war? |
| TILLY: | No. Loads of jobs going though; if you fancy a bit of work? |
| KATHERINE: | I don't think he'd like it. |
| TILLY: | What's it gotta do with him? |
| KATHERINE: | He won't like me earning my own money. |
| TILLY: | So don't tell him. |
| KATHERINE: | I couldn't. |
| TILLY: | I don't know why to stay with him Kath, he treats you like dirt. |
| KATHERINE: | He's a good man really Tilly. |
| TILLY: | So's Mussolini. |
| KATHERINE: | It's not as easy as you think. |
| TILLY: | What are you doing tomorrow night? |
| KATHERINE: | Tomorrow, why? |
| TILLY: | Me and a few of the girls are going to see the new Garbo movie. |
| KATHERINE: | Anna Karenina? |
| TILLY: | Have you seen it? |
| KATHERINE: | I've read the book. |
| TILLY: | Made it into a book already have they? Blimey. Anyhow do you fancy it? |
| KATHERINE: | I don't know… |

TILLY:           If it's too expensive Howard can get you in the fire doors, he knows the projectionist.

KATHERINE:    It's not the cost, its…

M. BOMULLOCK:  (*Appearing suddenly at the door*) Katherine, it's time to come in now.

KATHERINE:    I was just…

M. BOMULLOCK:  Now.

*Sheepishly KATHERINE goes back into the house, past MOTHER BOMULLOCK.*

TILLY:           Afternoon Mrs. Bomullock.

M. BOMULLOCK:  Hmm.

*MOTHER BOMULLOCK exits.*

### Brick by Brick (Reprise)
Brick by brick,
Brick by brick,
Brick by brick…

Every day,
The houses leapt up,
To try and scare away,
Reminders of the country.

Brick by brick,
Brick by brick,
Brick by brick…

## SCENE SIX:   The Front Garden of Anne Hurst's House - Late March 1936

*HURST stands, shouting up at a window.   A CROWD is gathering to watch the spectacle.*

HURST:  Anne!   Anne, come down here at once!   I know you're up there.

*A shy and rather worried servant (JANE) comes out of the house.*

JANE:  I'm afraid she's poorly Mr. Hurst, she asked me to convey her apologies...

HURST:  Poorly?  Poorly!  Oh, the time it takes to count her money must be tiring, exhausting no less?  For God's sake woman I can see her at the curtain!  Has she not got the decency to speak to her own father?

JANE:  She said she will be happy to speak with you another day.

HURST:  Is it the cart before the horse now then? Should I ask her permission on what I do? Anne!!

JANE:  Please sir, people are beginning to stare.

HURST:  Let them, let them stare.  Your neighbour, your neighbour my friends, has thrown her own father on to the streets.  Her own father! What do you say to that?  Is that any way for a 'respectable lady of the village' to behave? Eh?  To cast aside her own flesh and blood at the drop of a hat, eh?

ANNE:  *(Off)*  Pa, please.

HURST:  Oh, she talks.   The ailing waif has the power of speech.

JANE:  I told him what you said ma'am.

HURST:  Run along nymph, the Gorgon has awoke.

ANNE:          Will you stop making a fool of yourself.

HURST:        Couldn't make more of a fool if I had a ton of cream and a cart load of gooseberries. To think I trusted you? We trusted you to keep the farm.

ANNE:          It was my half.

HURST:        You had no intention of keeping it going…

ANNE:          Oh, be realistic. Wake up and smell the roses. There is no future in farming.

HURST:        Not without any land there ain't; people will always need food.

ANNE:          People need houses.

HURST:        Then why have you thrown us out on our ear?

ANNE:          We haven't thrown anyone out.

HURST:        Oh, it's 'we' now is it? Your new husband's making the decisions is he? I've seen the plans, there's no farm house on those plans. No room for anything between those houses.

ANNE:          You don't need such a large house.

HURST:        That is our home. Me and Agnes have a right to stay there.

ANNE:          Agnes?

HURST:        At least I have one daughter left, who wouldn't sell her own father down the Shuttle. I'm keeping that house, if I have to move it brick by brick, I will.

ANNE:          And where will you move it to?

HURST:        We still have half a farm in the family.

*AGNES enters, with ANNE's new husband EDD, slightly flustered at the sight of HURST.*

AGNES:        What are you doing here pa?

HURST:        (*To Edd*) Get your filthy hands off my daughter, isn't it enough that you've sucked the charity out of one?

EDD:        Now Mr. Hurst…

HURST:        Don't you 'Mr.' me. Don't you anything me. Come down from London with your plans and your fancy cars, think you can have anything you want...

EDD:        I'm merely a speculator, like yourself; sewing a few seeds.

HURST:        You are nothing like me, boy. Nor will you ever be. Come on Agnes, we've got enough manure to deal with at home.

        *HURST shepherds a bewildered AGNES off.*

EDD:        (*To ANNE*) She hasn't told him?

ANNE:        How can you reason with that?

EDD:        Run along Jane and get the tea ready would you, there's a good girl.

        *EDD looks down the road after HURST. The CROWD disperse.*

## Step Up

Come on, step up and be entertained,
Kick the blues from your shoes and be happy
again,
Take your mind off the times and sing a
cheerful refrain,
Come on, step up and be entertained.

Why think about life and how you should
complain,
When a play saves the day and stops you going
insane,
Let the actor distract ya and busy your brain,
Come on, step up and be entertained.

*(Fade)*       Come on, step up and be entertained,
Come on, step up and be entertained,
Come on, step up and be entertained…

## SCENE SEVEN:   Long Lane, Bexleyheath - Late March
## 1936

*The road has not been completely developed for*
*housing yet and as a result is fairly wooded, still*
*resembling a country lane.*

IRIS:         ...I'd have been inclined to tell him what to
              do with his bread.

BEA:          It's not that easy Iris.   You don't know what
              he's like indoors.

TILLY:        The rest of the street does, you can hear him at
              all hours.

MAY:          And she says nothing?

TILLY:        Not a peep.   And his mother's either in it with
              him, or turns a blind eye.

GINNY:        Either way's just as bad.

BEA:          Maybe she's scared of him too.

GINNY:        Of her own son?

BEA:          (*Giving an excellent impersonation*)  'It is
              written that there are only two perfectly good
              men – one dead, the other unborn.'

TILLY:        Mae West, Klondike Annie.

BEA:          Very good.

MAY:          Well I think I'd get a divorce.   They've added
              cruelty, insanity and drunkenness as grounds
              these days.

GINNY:        She could get three divorces then.

BEA:          Haven't you talked to her about it?

TILLY:        I've tried, but all she says is:  'It's not as easy
              as it seems'.   I don't like to keep on, in case
              she thinks I'm being nosy.

| | |
|---|---|
| IRIS: | Maybe she doesn't want anyone interfering. |
| GINNY: | Maybe she's happy. |
| BEA: | 'I want to be alone'. |
| MAY: | Gretta Garbo. |
| TILLY: | Grand Hotel. |
| GINNY: | You should have dressed up Bea, we might have all got in for nothing. |
| IRIS: | Why are you always doing impressions of people Bea? |
| BEA: | It's good practice for my voice. Who's this: 'Let's have less jawing and more boring'? |
| TILLY: | Mr. Hastings? |
| IRIS: | How am I supposed to guess that? I don't even work at Vickers. |
| MAY: | Don't know what you're missing. |
| TILLY: | Bea's hoping to work at the BBC. |
| IRIS: | Do you think anyone wants to hear a female voice on the wireless? |
| TILLY: | What about Jasmine Bligh? |
| MAY: | Or Elizabeth Cowell? |
| GINNY: | My old man says, if he wanted to listen to a woman's voice he'd take the cotton wool out of his ears at tea time. He says he only pays the licence fee to save having a conversation with me. |
| IRIS: | (*Mumbling*) Well I know what I'd do with his tea. |
| BEA: | 'Open your mouth when you are speaking, else it will heal up'. That's Madam Cooper. |

IRIS:        Madam Cooper?

BEA:         'Professional Contralto from West End
             Concert Halls. Twenty-five years teaching
             experience, moderate fees per lesson or per
             term.' She's only in Longlands Road. She
             'renders the voice mellow, free and of great
             carrying power'.

MAY:         Given up her 'West End' career then?

BEA:         She's got pictures, of her as a girl; must have
             been on a potato diet ever since mind, she
             could give a Zeppelin a run for it's money
             now.

IRIS:        How can you afford it?

BEA:         She does reduced rates for children of ex-
             servicemen. Anyway it's an investment:
             Once you're in at the BBC you're made.

TILLY:       You'll be able to do a feature on me, when I'm
             a famous film star.

GINNY:       We'll definitely be sitting in the circle at the
             picture house then.

TILLY:       What's that other one you do Bea? She knows
             the whole thing… That film they banned at
             Beckenham 'cause it was too scary?

IRIS:        King Kong?

TILLY:       That's the one.

BEA:         (*Striking a pose*) 'Ladies and gentlemen, I'm
             here tonight to tell you a very strange story – a
             story so strange that no one will believe it –
             but, ladies and gentlemen, seeing is believing.
             And we – my partners and I – have brought
             back the living proof of our adventure, an
             adventure in which twelve of our party met
             horrible deaths. And now, ladies and
             gentlemen, before I tell you any more, I'm

going to show you the greatest thing your eyes have ever beheld. He was a king in the world he knew, but now he comes to civilisation merely a captive – a show to gratify your curiosity. Ladies and gentlemen, look at Kong – the eighth wonder of the world!'

*HOWARD and BERTIE leap out of the bushes.*

HOWARD/BERTIE:   GRRRRAAAAHHH!!!

*The women scream, bumping into each other, as they turn to run and knock IRIS onto the floor. As they turn back to help her they see HOWARD.*

TILLY:          Howard!

BERTIE:         (*To Iris*))  Are you alright?

HOWARD:         Evening Iris.  I know you always wanted to fly but…

IRIS:           If you've ruined this dress you can buy me another.

TILLY:          Of all the stupid…

HOWARD:         Thought it was the Manor House Ghost did you?  Told you they would.  This is Bertie, he's a local.

MAY:            That explains a lot.

HOWARD:         He works at a signwriters in Bexley Heath, might be able to get me some work.

GINNY:          You leaving Vickers?

HOWARD:         Fed up with coming home filthy dirty.

IRIS:           They reckon he might be an ex-serviceman.

BERTIE:         Who?

IRIS:           The Manor House Ghost.

HOWARD:         'Ex' as in, de-mobbed or 'ex' as in <u>deceased</u>?

- 48 -

IRIS: That's when they first saw him, when Frognal became Queen Mary's. They used to deal with all the burns victims and that, from the Great War.

HOWARD: So?

IRIS: So, they didn't all make it, did they? Some of those pilots probably saw some horrific crashes.

HOWARD: I ain't ever heard anyone say he's wearing a flying helmet and goggles.

BERTIE: Didn't have a Manor House Ghosts before you Londoners came down.

HOWARD: You saying we brought him with us?

BEA: You don't believe he exists then Bertie?

BERTIE: I don't believe in nothing coming back from the dead.

MAY: Smokey Joe's seen him, he's a local.

BERTIE: Smokey Joe's seen White Elephants dancing down the Broadway.

TILLY: (*To Howard*) How did your meeting with the bank manager go?

HOWARD: Very well. In fact I've already been talking to Bertie here about a name for the Ball Room.

BERTIE: And a slogan.

BEA: So it's all going ahead?

HOWARD: Seems to be. I'm looking at a sight at the bottom of the park, 'Little Danson' it's called. Most of the estate's been sold off, but the house is still there. Takes up a fair bit of ground, enough to build a dance hall on. The yard's being used by a local builders.

GINNY: Well they ain't going to be in a hurry to sell up are they?

HOWARD: I wouldn't be so sure, a lot of the local boys are being squeezed out by the big firms, they don't need local sand and brick pits 'cause they can import it cheaper from abroad.

BERTIE: They reckon the government's got plans to slow up the building anyway, Green Belt and Braces or something.

HOWARD: Can't see that happening, not with the amount of work it's brought in.

TILLY: Not with the queues of labourers at Blackfen.

MAY: Are they going to let you build right on the edge of the park?

HOWARD: They'll let you build anywhere if you've got the money. Look how much open space there is.

GINNY: So why build it there then?

HOWARD: Because that is the main road to and from London, the foot of Shooters Hill, it's ideal.

BEA: Do we all get in free then Howie?

HOWARD: Leave it out, I've got to pay my loan back somehow.

TILLY: How long will it be before you can open?

HOWARD: Well the house is no good, might as well start again there.

BERTIE: That's a nice old house that.

HOWARD: Got to be practical Bertie, it ain't no dance hall. I reckon with the demolition and the re-building you're looking at six months.

MAY: Just in time for Christmas.

HOWARD:     Yeah.   Better start looking for a band, some of
            them are probably booked up already; can't
            have a dance hall with no music.

### Step Up

Come on, step up and be entertained,
Kick the blues from your shoes and be happy
again,
Take your mind off the times and sing a
cheerful refrain,
Come on, step up and be entertained.

Why be alone with your world in decay,
When a partner could start yer to thinking OK,
Let the beat treat your feet to dance your
troubles away,
Come on, step up and be entertained.

Come on, step up and be entertained,
Kick the blues from your shoes and be happy
again,
Take your mind off the times and sing a
cheerful refrain,
Come on, step up and be entertained.

Why sit there at home with your and worries
all day,
When those silver screen idols can keep them
at bay,
Let the movies move you and take you away,
Come on, step up and be entertained.

Come on, step up and be entertained,
Kick the blues from your shoes and be happy
again,
Take your mind off the times and sing a
cheerful refrain,
Come on, step up and be entertained.

And if ever you feel those blues again,
Come on, step up and be entertained.

HOWARD:     Come on Till, I'll race you to the picture
            house.

*They all run off, except for IRIS who realises she has
dropped her bag.   BERTIE comes back for her.*

BERTIE:     Are you alright?

IRIS:       Yes, I dropped my bag.

BERTIE:     Oh.  Look, I'm sorry we frightened you, it was
            Howard's idea.

IRIS:       I wouldn't worry about it, I've known Howard
            long enough to recognise one of his ideas when
            it knocks you over.

BERTIE:     He seems very erm…

IRIS:       Stupid?

BERTIE:     Impetuous.

IRIS:       That's a big word for a country bumpkin.

BERTIE:     We don't all have a piece of straw sticking out
            of our mouths you know.

IRIS:       I know.  I see some of you are wearing shoes
            and socks as well now.

BERTIE:     And I hear that they're teaching you lot to eat
            with a knife and fork?

IRIS:       Only on Sundays.  I'm sorry.  It just feels like
            I'm stuck in the middle of nowhere sometimes.

BERTIE:     Whereabouts do you live?

IRIS:       Sidcup.

BERTIE:     You are.

IRIS:       Thanks.

BERTIE:     Do you work at Vickers with the others?

IRIS:      No. We know each other from the East End.
           I'm a nurse at Queen Mary's.

BERTIE:    Oh, that's how you knew about Frognal?
           Thought it was a bit strange for a Londoner to
           know anything about anything round here.

IRIS:      Have you always lived here?

BERTIE:    Country boy born and bread, strong in the arm
           and thick in the head.

IRIS:      So this is where you'll marry, have children
           and die?

BERTIE:    Far from it. I'm going to live in Florida.

IRIS:      Florida?

BERTIE:    It's in America - where they hold the speed
           trials for the fastest car in the world.

IRIS:      Bluebird?

BERTIE:    How do you know that?

IRIS:      So what are you planning to do: Paint the
           'stop' sign?

BERTIE:    I'm going to be a driver, like Malcolm
           Campbell.

IRIS:      Good for you.

BERTIE:    Ha. Most people say 'isn't that a bit
           dangerous'.

IRIS:      Malcolm Campbell seems to know what he's
           doing.

BERTIE:    That's right. And when your number's up,
           that's it. Doesn't matter how careful you are.

IRIS:      I like that. You know what I want to be?

BERTIE:    Florence Nightingale?

- 53 -

| | |
|---|---|
| IRIS: | A pilot, like Amy Johnson. |
| BERTIE: | My old man wanted to be a pilot. |
| IRIS: | What stopped him? |
| BERTIE: | The Somme. |
| IRIS: | I'm sorry. |
| BERTIE: | I think that's where I get my thirst for excitement. |
| IRIS: | You don't fancy flying? |
| BERTIE: | Not fast enough for me, Bluebird's gone over 300 miles per hour, you won't get a plane doing that. Anyway why aren't you working at Vickers, if you're so interested in flying? Their Vimmy was the first plane across the Atlantic. |
| IRIS: | They're more interested in making war machinery now. Why don't you work at a garage? |
| BERTIE: | I'm not interested in fixing other people's cars. |
| IRIS: | There we are then. It's too easy to get distracted, life's too short. |
| BERTIE: | And hospital work isn't a distraction? |
| IRIS: | At least I can feel I'm doing something worthwhile, until I've got some savings behind me. |
| BERTIE: | I've got my driving test in a couple of months. |
| IRIS: | Can I be your first passenger? |
| BERTIE: | Only if I can be yours. |

*They exit toward the cinema arm in arm.*

### **Boom (Reprise)**

Boom, boom, boom,
Boom, boom, boom,
Boom, boom, boom, boom, boom.

Boom, boom, boom,
Boom, boom, boom,
Boom, boom, boom, boom, boom.

## SCENE EIGHT:   The Bexleyheath and District Laundry – April 1936

*Outside the massive laundry shed some of the girls are having a break.  From inside the washroom the clatter of the machines can be heard.  AGNES approaches, holding a bundle of sheets.*

AGNES:      Do you work here?

RUTH:       No, we always dress like this.

AGNES:      Don't be insolent to me young lady, I have a complaint.

ISOBEL:     It's a doctor that you want then love.

*The girls giggle.*

AGNES:      I wish to speak with your supervisor.

RUTH:       We're on a break.

AGNES:      I don't care if you're on the last lifeboat of the Titanic.

ISOBEL:     (*Sighs*) She's in there.

AGNES:      I do not wish to go 'in there', it's too awful. Fetch her out here at once.

RUTH:       But…

AGNES:      Do I need to speak to the manager?

RUTH:       Alright, alright.  (*Shouting off*)  Sarah, Sarah! Someone wants to see you.  Someone wants to see you.  Yes.  Out here; some woman.

*SARAH appears.*

SARAH:      Yes, can I help you?

AGNES:      I should hope so.  These are not my sheets.

SARAH:      Oh, well if you'd like to come in…

AGNES:      No I should not like to come in.

SARAH:      Well I just need to…

AGNES:      All I require are my own sheets and I shall be
            on my way.

SARAH:      Did they have your name on them?

AGNES:      Of course they had my name on them.

SARAH:      But these aren't yours?

AGNES:      I've just told you they're not mine, haven't I?
            I know my own sheets when I see them.

SARAH:      Well I can't see how they could have got
            mixed up…

AGNES:      Then perhaps you should see.   Perhaps you
            should go and get me my sheets and take these
            one's back to wherever they came from.

SARAH:      When were they delivered?

AGNES:      This morning.

SARAH:      Ah, well the van's not back yet.   I can't do
            anything 'till the van's back.

AGNES:      Why?

SARAH:      Because then I'll know if there's been a mix
            up.

AGNES:      Well obviously there's been a mix up…   You
            mean someone else may have my sheets?

SARAH:      It stands to reason doesn't it, unless they're on
            the van still.

AGNES:      Someone else has <u>my</u> sheets?

SARAH:      Naturally we'd wash them again, if that's the
            case.

AGNES:     That's not the point, is it?   Who knows what they might have done on them.

*ALICE has appeared from the washroom, wearing the white overalls of the other wash girls.*

ALICE:     Agnes?

AGNES:     Alice?   What are you doing here?

ALICE:     I work here.

AGNES:     Here?

SARAH:     Do you two know each other?

ALICE:     This is my sister, Agnes.

ISOBEL:    Oh,… her.

AGNES:     What do you mean 'her'.

ISOBEL:    Nothing.

ALICE:     Is it true, what I've heard?

AGNES:     I wish to speak to the manager.

SARAH:     I'm afraid he's on his lunch break at the moment.

ALICE:     Agnes?

AGNES:     Then I wish to speak to whoever's in charge.

SARAH:     That's me.

ALICE:     Agnes, is it true?

AGNES:     Not now Alice.

ALICE:     I need to know.

RUTH:      What's the matter, don't want to wash your dirty laundry in public?

| | |
|---|---|
| AGNES: | (*Clearly put out by the remark*)  Excuse me a minute, would you. |

*AGNES takes ALICE to one side.*

| | |
|---|---|
| AGNES: | Look Alice, I'm sorry you have to work in a place like this but don't be so familiar in front of those sort of girls.   They need to understand respect. |
| ALICE: | Respect? |
| AGNES: | Yes. |
| ALICE: | For you? |
| AGNES: | Of course. |
| ALICE: | From what I've heard you don't deserve any respect. |
| AGNES: | And what have you heard? |
| ALICE: | That you've sold up the farm between you, turned Dad out of the house, that you're having an affair with your sister's new husband. |

*AGNES gasps.*

| | |
|---|---|
| AGNES: | Who told you that? |
| ALICE: | Oh come off it, don't you think anyone else goes to the Regal? |
| AGNES: | Have you...? |
| ALICE: | Not me, I can't afford it on my wages. |
| AGNES: | Eddy and I are simply good friends, that's all. |
| ALICE: | I don't care about that.   It's Dad I care about. |
| AGNES: | Oh, he'll come round.   He's got somewhere to live already:  One of the hutments over at East Wickham. |

ALICE:           Those shacks?  How could you?

*In the background HOWARD has arrived carrying a large basket of washing.*

HOWARD:          (*To the others*)  Afternoon ladies, the Vickers' laundry's here.

AGNES:           He couldn't live with us, it would be impossible.

ALICE:           The least you could do is let him keep the farm house.

AGNES:           You can't plan around an old building, any developer knows that.  What use is that dilapidated old thing stuck in the middle of an estate?

ALICE:           It's not yours to sell.

AGNES:           Oh but it is, we have the deeds.

ALICE:           You swindled those out of him.

AGNES:           You better watch your mouth Alice Hurst.  Or else you might find yourself the subject of a letter of complaint to your boss.

ALICE:           Really?  I'd best make it worth your while then hadn't I?

*ALICE knocks the sheet from her hand and treads it into the mud defiantly.  AGNES smirks.*

AGNES:           (*Smug*)  Not my sheets.

*AGNES turns to walk away, ALICE leaps towards her and pulls her hat down over her eyes, tearing the seams. She then starts to fight with AGNES.*

SARAH:           No fighting with the customers, no fighting with the customers!

RUTH:            Give her what for Alice!

HOWARD:          Ladies, ladies please!

ALICE:          You wait 'till I tell Anne you're seeing her
                husband.

AGNES:          Oh please, do you think she's got any interest
                in what you have to say? You're just sore
                because you talked yourself out of the farm.

ALICE:          I was trying to be honest! At least I'd have
                tried to make a go of it.

*AGNES composes herself and dusts herself off.*

AGNES:          I paid good money for this hat.

ALICE:          You haven't got any good money.

*AGNES launches herself at ALICE, while HOWARD
tries to keep them apart.*

HOWARD:         Feel free to help me someone.

*MR. DRAY, the manager returns from lunch.*

DRAY:           What the hell is going on here!!

SARAH:          Afternoon Mr. Dray.

DRAY:           (*To Agnes*) Who are you?

AGNES:          I am an ex-customer. I simply came to make a
                complaint...

RUTH:           She did not...

ISOBEL:         She's a jezebel...

DRAY:           Quiet!! Have you a complaint with the
                service?

AGNES:          I have a complaint with the sort you choose to
                employ.

DRAY:           If you have a complaint, there are ways to deal
                with it. I do not expect physical abuse to my
                staff. If you would care to write to me

- 61 -

regarding the matter I will be happy to deal with it.  Sarah, give the lady my details would you?  Now please Sarah.

SARAH: Yes Mr. Dray.  (*Then to Agnes*)  Come this way please.

*AGNES and SARAH exit.*

ISOBEL: Well done Mr. Dray.

DRAY: Ruth, get Alice's belongings.

RUTH: But...

DRAY: Fetch them now, or fetch your own with them.

*RUTH exits.*

DRAY: I do not employ street brawling harlots, Miss Hurst.  I'll send the boy to your lodgings with the remainder of your wages.

HOWARD: With all due respect Mr. Dray...

DRAY: This is nothing to do with you Howard.  Finish up your break and come inside Isobel.

*MR. DRAY exits.*

ISOBEL: That is so unfair.  You should go and tell him that she's your sister.

HOWARD: Your sister?

ALICE: It's a long story.

*RUTH returns with a bundle of ALICE's possessions.*

RUTH: She's in there now, giving it the old water works.

ISOBEL: What will you do Alice?

ALICE: Look for another job.

ISOBEL: But Mrs. Travis won't have you lodging there, if she finds out you've been given the sack; especially if she finds out it's for fighting.

RUTH: So don't tell her.

HOWARD: You could find a better job than this.

RUTH: Thanks.

HOWARD: I mean, tell your landlady you've given in your notice – when you've got another job to go to.

ISOBEL: Here, they must need people at Vickers Howard.

HOWARD: Sure to, it's dirty work mind.

ALICE: As long as it pays the rent.

HOWARD: I'll ask my sister, she's on the assembly line.

RUTH: Don't worry Ali, we'll make sure old snotty draws' sheets get shredded in the dryer.

ISOBEL: If they ever turn up.

HOWARD: Can I drop you off anywhere? I've got the van out front.

ALICE: Yes, thank you. Are you going anywhere near East Wickham?

HOWARD: I'm on company time and petrol, we can go anywhere you like.

## Brick by Brick (Reprise)

Brick by brick,
Brick by brick,
Brick by brick…

One Dark night,
A farmer crept out,
And under the moon light,
Prepared to say goodnight.

Brick by brick,
Brick by brick,
Brick by brick….

## SCENE NINE:   Outside Hurst's Empty Farmhouse – April 1936

> *HURST stands alone.   Close by he has a large metal jerry can.*

HURST:  So, this is the last Spring.   Who knows what will stand here by next year.   No green shoots, no thick earth hugging at your boots. Seasons'll just be 'weather' to those who sleep tight, protected from the real land by concrete: Fending off nature behind a fortress of sharp pebbledash.   No-one'll remember old Hurst, who worked all his life to feed his family, feed the City - that now chokes the very hand… They've deserted me Bess, all three of them left, like rats off a sinking ship.   What will become of this old place?   This house which gave life to them all?   These walls - soaked in memories - witness to the ebb and flow of past lives, will be cracked and scattered like old bones ready for the Gypsy cart.   I can't let them steal away the last breath of air.   Or gently put to rest the stack of reminders that you inhale on opening the door.   I ain't done for yet Bess, there's a spark of fight left in this old frame, girl.

> *HURST opens the can and begins to pour the liquid around the floor, then onto his own clothing.   He tosses the empty can aside and takes out a box of matches.*

HURST:  Should be enough, with what I've already done.   I'll be coming home soon Bess, and leaving them ashes for their foundations.

> *HURST strikes the match but it does not light.   He tries again, still nothing.   A HOODED FIGURE, with a hidden white face appears up stage.   HURST tries again, still no luck.   The HOODED FIGURE moves towards him.   HURST sees the FIGURE but still frantically tries to light the match.*

HURST:  (*Thinking the figure is the Grim Reaper*)   No, no, not yet, I'm not ready.   Leave me be 'til I'm done here!

*The match lights.*

HURST:          I'll choose when I'm ready.

*The FIGURE blows out the match.*

## SCENE TEN:   The Bank of the Sidcup Bypass – May 1936

*Throughout the scene people arrive with picnic baskets,*
*deck chairs and drinks to spend the afternoon watching*
*the traffic go by.   RUTH, ISOBEL and SARAH sit*
*together as do MARY, JANE and DOT.   The*
*CHILDREN are out for the day with the MISTRESS.*

MISTRESS:        Children, this is the Sidcup Bypass.   It has
been built for the London traffic and takes you
right into London, or eventually will go right
out to the coast.   You may play on the bank
here, but I don't want to see anyone going near
the road.   Now, while I read my book, feel
free to have fun.   But, if anyone starts to play
up we will be going straight back and you will
lose your Sunday privileges for three weeks.
Do I make myself clear?

CHILDREN:        Yes Miss.

MISTRESS:        Very well, then off you go.

### Watching The Cars Go By

People drift by in cars,
                        Take your seats,
And I ain't going nowhere.
                        Turn the key,
Towards a brand new start,
                        Join the flow,
A tide of tarmac flowing.
                        Ride the waves,
                        drift away.


There's miles of road,
                        We like the road,
But I'm stuck here at home.
                        Can't wait to get
                        out,
I've got a full tank of fuel,
                        Burn the fuel,
And I just can't seem to roam.
                        Hit the gas, cruise
                        away, let's go.

- 67 -

When young I had a dream,
                    Follow dreams,
But dreams can sear to ashes,
                    Burn them bright,
Along life's torrid stream,
                    Learn to sail,
Survival's where the catch is.
                    Use your skills to
                    endure.

There's miles of road,
                    We like the road,
But I'm stuck here at home.
                    Can't wait to get
                    out,
I've got a full tank of fuel,
                    Burn the fuel,
And I just can't seem to roam.
                    Hit the gas, cruise
                    away, let's go.

I'm at the side of the street,
                    Start your engines,
And the traffic rushes by.
                    Hit the gas, cruise
                    away, let's go.

*The SHANKS GANG are installed on the warm grass*
*verge, guessing which make of car passes.*
*SOUND of a car passing.*

SHANKS:     Wolseley.

JOE:        That was never a Wolseley.

SHANKS:     'Course it was.

JOE:        It was a Major saloon.

CHARLIE:    Oxford.

GRACE:      Don't be daft the Oxford hasn't got the suicide
            doors at the back.

CHARLIE:    Niether's the new Major.

GRACE: Then it's an old Major isn't it?

SHANKS: It is a Wolseley.

FLO: I don't know how you can tell the difference with these new cars, they all look the same to me.

SHANKS: Well that was a Wolseley.

CHARLIE: Oxford.

*Cars continue to pass as...*

FLO: I'm getting bored here.

KID: I thought we was going fishing?

FLO: I hate fishing, all that waiting around for hours.

CHARLIE: Not that sort of fishing.

JOE: Dry land fishing, see what we can catch around here?

KID: (*Disappointed*) Oh thieving? I brought me rod and all.

JOE: Shhhh.

SHANKS: Fishing season's over.

JOE: What you on about?

SHANKS: We ain't fishing any more.

CHARLIE: We're going straight? I just bought a suit on the never never.

SHANKS: 'Course we ain't going straight.

JOE: So how are we going to make money then?

SHANKS: Racketeering.

KID: We're going to make sports stuff?

JOE:           I thought Chaz was the stupid one.

CHARLIE:     Yeah.  Hang on...

SHANKS:      What's the point of making money the hard way, when you can make it the easy way? You don't need to sell stuff, just look after it – like Big Al.

GRACE:       Who?

SHANKS:      Capone.

JOE:           Isn't he in prison?

SHANKS:      Well, at the moment yes.  Look, all he does is offer protection: 'insurance'.

KID:           I don't wanna be an insurance man Shank. It's all figures and that.

SHANKS:      All we have to do is approach local businesses and offer them protection against vandalism, that sort of thing:  Against gangs coming and smashing up the place.

CHARLIE:     Sounds a bit... dangerous.  Sort of 'James Cagney'.

SHANKS:      We are the gangs Charlie, there ain't anyone else organised around here.  A few kids we can clip round the ear, that's it.  We'll be laughing.

JOE:           So we offer protection against other gangs...

SHANKS:      But there aren't any, so we're quids in.

KID:           And I don't have to crawl through any more broken windows?

FLO:           And we can be gangster's Molls?

SHANKS:      Yeah, whatever you say.  So, are you in?

*SHANKS puts his hand in the middle of the group and the others place their hands on top, showing agreement. While they have been talking BOMULLOCK, his MOTHER and KATHERINE have arrived, Katherine carrying a large picnic basket. They set the basket down and start to unpack it.*

MARY: …but I don't see what you've got against going into service.

DOT: It's degrading, isn't it.

JANE: Depends who you work for.

MARY: I earn far more than you do at the sign writers.

JANE: And Bertie ain't interested in you Dot.

DOT: The only thing he's interested in are his stupid cars.

JANE: Further more you get all the gossip when you're in service.

MARY: Yeah, but you get a better class of gossip working for a Lady: more staff.

JANE: But you ain't heard the latest: The sister, Agnes, is planning to run off with him – the husband.

MARY: No.

JANE: It's true. Once he's had the land signed over to him he's going to give Anne the elbow and shack up with her. I heard them in the kitchen the other day. Mind you he's probably only after the old farm, once he's got that he'll ditch them both.

DOT: So where does that leave you?

JANE: I hadn't thought of that.

*TILLY and the others arrive, with LUCY and ALICE.*

IRIS:      This is it?

BERTIE:    Yeah, we come up here on a Sundays and
           watch the traffic.

IRIS:      Bertie, when you said 'I'll take you out at the
           weekend' this wasn't quite what I had in mind.

HOWARD:    Oh stop moaning Iris, it's as good a place as
           any.

ALICE:     This was Hobland's Wood, when my dad was
           a boy, couldn't drive a cart through here then.

BERTIE:    Hmmm, smell those petrol fumes eh?

LUCY:      They make me feel sick.

BERTIE:    Bit of petrol never hurt anyone.

MAY:       Get those sandwiches out, I'm famished.

BERTIE:    (*To Iris*)  I've got a surprise for you.

IRIS:      What is it?

BERTIE:    Well it wouldn't be a surprise if I told you,
           would it?

*The WOMEN from the laundry see ALICE for the first
time.*

RUTH:      Alice?

ALICE:     Ruth, how are you?

RUTH:      Same as ever, but what about you?

ALICE:     Oh I'm fine, Howard managed to get me an
           office job down at the Vickers' works.

SARAH:     Probably the best thing that ever happened to
           you, losing your job at the laundry.  You've
           got a good head on your shoulders, it's about
           time you used it.

ISOBEL:    So you didn't tell Mrs. Travis then?

ALICE:       Well, actually I'm sharing a room with Tilly
             and Lucy, only until I get myself straight.

ISOBEL:      Ooo, I see.

ALICE:       No, it's nothing like that.

RUTH:        And what's this I hear about you opening a
             dance hall, Howard?

HOWARD:      Blimey it hasn't taken long for that to get
             around.

RUTH:        I hope you're planning on having a celebrity
             down to open it?

SARAH:       Yeah, like Fred Astair.

HOWARD:      It's not opening until December, it's not even
             built yet.

SARAH:       Hey that's good, I'll book now for our firms
             Christmas knees up.

HOWARD:      Great.

*The SHANKS gang have spotted another car.*

SHANKS:      There's the new Jag.

JOE:         It's an MG.

SHANKS:      I know a Jag when I see one.

*Two GYPSIES enter, selling lucky heather, along with
some GYPSY children. As the scene progresses the two
groups of children start to annoy each other. The two
GYPSIES approach BOMULLOCK.*

GYPSY:       Lucky heather?

BOMULLOCK: Clear off.

TELLER:      Fortunes? Read your palm?

BOMULLOCK: I can tell you your fortune, if you don't hop it. Now sling yer hook.

*The GYPSIES move on.*

BOMULLOCK: (Taking the paper from a pie)  What's this?

KATHERINE: A pork pie.

BOMULLOCK: Did I ask for pork?

KATHERINE: No, but you have one every day.

BOMULLOCK: Yeah, I have one every day.  Then didn't it occur to you that perhaps on a Sunday I might want something else?  Did that thought not cross your tiny brain?

GINNY: Look, he's at it again.

TILLY: Oh, I've got so used to it I don't even notice any more.

HOWARD: One of these day's I'm going to give him what for.

TILLY: And make it worse for her?

LUCY: I'll stick a jar of dad's bees in his trousers.

BEA: (Raising her glass)  'To new worlds of Gods and Monsters'.

IRIS: Not now Bea.

TILLY: Ernest Thesiger – Bride of Frankenstein.

BEA: Oh, you're good.

TILLY: (To pacify the others)  It's nothing to do with us, alright?

BOMULLOCK: I thought maybe for once you could use your own initiative.  Go back home and get me a steak and kidney, don't whine woman, just do as I say.

*KATHERINE looks to MOTHER BOMULLOCK but she
turns away. KATHERINE goes to fetch another pie.*

BOMULLOCK: Honestly mother, I sometimes wonder if we
made the right choice.

M BOMULLOCK: (*Distant*) So do I.

*LADY KNOTCHEL enters, accompanied by
GREENBAG, she has been walking her dog.*

GYPSY: Lucky heather your ladyship?

TELLER: Read your palm ma'am?

*LADY KNOTCHEL ignores them and continues on her
way.*

GREENBAG: ...but the problem is, any developer would
have the cost of demolishing the house.

KNOTCHEL: But I'm not asking you the price of the land
Mr. Greenbag, it's the house I wish to sell.

GREENBAG: That's what I'm trying to explain your
ladyship, it's why none of the big housing
agents have been interested - no one wants
manor houses.

KNOTCHEL: Nonsense, people shall always want large
houses.

GREENBAG: But not here, not in the middle of suburbia.
You can buy an 'A' type chalet house in
Sidcup for £695, that's eighteen shillings a
week on the mortgage – three bedrooms, drive,
garage, hundred foot garden. That's what
people want 'round here. When your family
bought your house it would have been classed
as a country residence. This is now commuter
belt. No one feels they can escape from it all
by coming to Bexley any more.

KNOTCHEL: Well I'm certainly not selling to developers,
who'll ruin the grounds and house twenty
families there.

GREENBAG:      Four times that at least.

KNOTCHEL:      (*Calling off, to the dog*)  Wellington.
               Wellington!

*The dog barks, off.*

KNOTCHEL:      Wellington, leave that man alone!

*Wellington is growling, off.*

HURST:         (*Off*)  Get off me, get off will you!

KNOTCHEL:      Wellington!

GYPSY:         (*To Bertie*)  Lucky heather?

BERTIE:        Go on then, we all need a bit of luck don't we?

TELLER:        (*To Howard*)  Read your palm love?

HOWARD:        Oh, why not?

*She starts to read his palm.*

HURST:         (*Off*)  Let go of me you mutt!

KNOTCHEL:      Wellington!  Oh, I do hate shouting.  Mary!
               Mary, thank heaven's you're here dear.
               Would you mind awfully, fetching
               Wellington?  He's got himself attached to that
               beggar.

DOT:           (To Mary)  Tell her to sod off, it's your day
               off.

SHANKS:        (*Excited by the man and dog fight*)  Go on my
               son, give him what for.

JOE:           I'll lay you a tenner on the dog.

*MARY reluctantly exits to separate them.*

JOE:           Hey, that's not fair, it's two against one.

| | |
|---|---|
| BERTIE: | (*To IRIS*) Right, surprise time. (*He kisses her on the cheek*) Don't go away. |

*IRIS looks puzzled as BERTIE exits in the opposite direction to the spectacle.*

| | |
|---|---|
| MAY: | What on earth is going on over there? |
| MARY: | (*Off*) Leave Wellington, leave! |
| KNOTCHEL: | Don't hurt him dear. |
| BEA: | Some dog trying to eat an old tramp. |
| GINNY: | Oh these stupid dogs, if they can't control them people shouldn't be allowed to have them. |
| MARY: | (*Off*) Bad dog, bad! |

*HURST staggers on, slightly bewildered.*

| | |
|---|---|
| MARY: | (*Off*) Come back here! Wellington come back! |
| KNOTCHEL: | (*To Hurst*) I do apologise, he's normally so well behaved. |
| IRIS: | (*Joking*) I wonder if this was Bertie's surprise? |
| LUCY: | He's scary Till. |
| TILLY: | He's only an old man Luce. |
| MAY: | More like a wild man. |
| ALICE: | (*Close to tears*) That's my father. |

*ALICE rushes over to him.*

| | |
|---|---|
| HOWARD: | Alice? |
| TELLER: | Hold still. (*Then to the Gypsy*) I don't like this Kit. |

*The second GYPSY looks over his palm for confirmation. She looks at her friend with trepidation. The following conversations overlap between groups. Turbulent threatening MUSIC starts to underscore the scene. The CHILDREN's play becomes more violent, some are fighting. The MISTRESS is too involved in her book to notice.*

HOWARD:      What? What is it?

TELLER:      Here, take your money back.

HOWARD:      I don't want it back.

KNOTCHEL:      (*To Hurst*) Don't I know you? It's Hurst isn't it?

HURST:      You don't know me, you can't.

ALICE:      Dad, dad it's me, Alice.

HURST:      Don't taunt me young lady! My Alice is dead.

TELLER:      (*To Howard*) The dead will rise.

HOWARD:      What?

BEA:      What's she going on about?

KNOTCHEL:      (*To Hurst*) You used to supply us with vegetables.

*There is a car horn and the roar of an engine as a car speeds past.*

JANE:      (*To Dot*) Hey look, it's Bertie.

DOT:      He must have passed his test.

JOE:      (*To Shanks*) What was that then?

SHANKS:      Didn't see it.

IRIS:      (*To Howard*) It's all rubbish this fortune telling.

CHARLIE:      (*To Shanks*) It was a BSA.

GRACE: That was never a BSA.

FLO: Driving like and idiot whoever it was.

GYPSY: (*To Howard*)  The ghost of the last war will return to haunt us once more.

HURST: (*To Alice*)  I've seen him, he came for me, but I was too quick.

ALICE: Dad?

HURST: Get your hands off me, you'll slow me up.

KNOTCHEL: What's the matter with him?

ALICE: I don't know.

> *The car horn sounds again, with the roar of an engine.*
> *DOT and JANE wave as the car rushes by, but IRIS is*
> *too involved to notice.*
> *MUSIC builds.*

JOE: (*To Shanks*)  Now that is a Wolseley.

SHANKS: No way.

CHARLIE: BSA I'm telling you.

TILLY: (*Aggressively, to Teller*)  What's that supposed to mean?  'The ghost of the last war will return to haunt us once more'?

GINNY: (*Worried*)  Is there going to be another war?

MAY: (*Dismissive*)  'Course not.

HOWARD: (*To Gypsies*)  Wait, wait.

IRIS: They're only saying it so you give them more money.

HOWARD: They gave me back my money

Darren Rapier

*BOMULLOCK, who has taken notice of what the
GYPSIES have said seems concerned by this. He grabs
the TELLER by the arm.*
*MUSIC builds.*

BOMULLOCK: (*To Teller*)  What did you say to him?  What
did you say!

HURST: (*To Knotchel*)  I can't stay, he'll find me, he'll
find me wherever I am.

KNOTCHEL: Hurst, Hurst?  Listen to me man.

ALICE: (*To Hurst*)  Wait, wait, I can help you.

GYPSY: (*To Bomullock*)  Leave her be, we ain't done
nothing to you.

HOWARD: (*To Teller*)  I want to know what it means?

BOMULLOCK: What did she say to you?

TELLER: Let me go.

HURST: (*To Alice*)  Let me go.

*The car roars past again, with a cacophony of hoots on
the hooter.  Finally IRIS looks up.*

SHANKS: He's a bloody lunatic.

BOMULLOCK: (*To Teller*)  What did you say about the
ghosts of the last war!?

*The TELLER breaks free.  HURST breaks free.*

GYPSY: (*To Teller*)  There's something bad about this
place.

*Eyes follow the GYPSIES and HURST, who meet centre
stage.  For a moment there is deadlock as each senses
something paranormal in the other.*
*The car roars past again, hooting.  This time IRIS
recognises BERTIE and smiles.*

*One of the CHILDREN snatches another's hat and
throws it  into the road.*

*The car is heard skidding.   DOT, IRIS and JANE's faces turn to expressions of horror and there is a loud CRASH, as vehicles hit each other.   All eyes face front towards the crash.*

IRIS/DOT:        BERTIE!!

*MUSIC swells to a crescendo.*

ALL:             BOOM!!

*Blackout.*
                            **INTERVAL**

**<u>SCENE ELEVEN</u>:   Danson Park – July 1936**

*The opening of the Danson park swimming pool.   In a
tent are various stalls, showing the latest in electrical
conveniences:   Wash tubs; Irons; Lighting; Heaters;
Towel warmers; Clocks; Exercise belts; Lit signs.
There is a large display of televisions.   Above the stalls
there is a sign saying 'THE ELECTRICAL ERA IS
HERE'.*

## The Age of Being at Home

There's danger in those footsteps,
As you walk out that door,
You can trip up on that black cat,
And tumble to the floor.
That ladder hangs there waiting,
For when you least suspect,
To find a falling hazard,
And break your dog gone neck.

Yeah, yeah, yeah,

Don't call me after dark babe,
I won't pick the phone,
I never get the front door,
Pretend I'm not at home.
I always leave the lights off,
Until I've drawn the blind,
If you're looking for a home bird,
That's exactly what you'd find.

Now you might think I'm crazy,
You might think I'm mad,
But the world's a big old place babe,
And it's a big old place that's bad.
You can fill a house with gadgets,
Which know exactly what to do,
And when it comes to good replacements,
There's even one for you!

This is the age of being at home,
It's an electric rendezvous.

*The CHILDREN are watching an IRON LADY demonstrating how to iron shirts.*

IRON LADY: The beauty of an electric iron is that it heats itself.

CHILD: Cor, can we get one of those?

MISTRESS: No.

CHILD: How can you iron properly with a chord attached to one end of your iron?

MISTRESS: Be quiet.

IRON LADY: Once heated the iron will stay at the set temperature until switched off.

*The SHANKS gang are milling about. DOREEN, the television sales lady, is distracted by a potential customer.*

SHANKS: Quick Kid, grab one of those.

KID: What's it for?

SHANKS: I don't know, but it looks like it's worth nicking.

*The KID grabs a television but it is heavier than he thought.*

KID: Shanks, Shanks it weighs a ton

CHARLIE: She's coming back.

KID: Help, I'm going to drop it!

SHANKS: Leg it!

*They run off in different directions. SHANKS bumps into HOWARD as he exits. Seeing THE KID struggling HOWARD helps him put the television back on the display.*

KID: Thanks mister.

- 83 -

*THE KID runs off as fast as he can, much to HOWARD's surprise.*

DOREEN: Oh, I see you're interested in the televisions?

HOWARD: No actually I'm just looking for my sister.

DOREEN: Well your sister is a very forward thinking lady. This slim line model is both light and attractive, with a large ten inch screen.

HOWARD: No, I mean I'm looking for my sis...

*TILLY, BEA, ALICE and, KATHERINE enter.*

TILLY: Here you are Howard, we've been looking for you everywhere, the swimming's about to start.

CHILDREN: Swimming!

IRON LADY: Mind the iron, mind the iron!

MISTRESS: Come back here!

*The CHILDREN rush out, past LADY KNOTCHEL and her two friends LADY WOOLWARD and LADY TULCHAN.*

TULCHAN: Really, the manners of these children.

WOOLWARD: Who did you say the polo match was between?

KNOTCHEL: Plumstead and Woolwich, but it's not until after the swimming gala, so we've got plenty of time.

BEA: (*To Howard*) They've got one of the women who are going to be swimming at the Berlin Olympics.

TILLY: You could ask her if she'd open the dance hall for you Howard?

HOWARD: Why would I want a swimmer opening the dance hall? You might as well ask Fred Perry.

BEA:            Yes please.

HOWARD:         No.   You need someone who can do a turn.

TILLY:          Ginger Rogers?

HOWARD:         Who I can afford.   Anyway, I've got someone
                in mind.

TILLY:          Who?

HOWARD:         Never you mind.   Her agent's getting back to
                me.

TILLY:          You'll tell us Alice?

ALICE:          I've been sworn to secrecy.

HOWARD:         Where's Lucy?

TILLY:          She's helping dad with his display.

KATHERINE:      (*Noticing the televisions*)   What's this?

DOREEN:         It's a wireless, with pictures.

BEA:            You what?

DOREEN:         These are televisions.

TILLY:          Oh I saw these in the paper, aren't the BBC
                doing something with them?

DOREEN:         Yes that's right, they'll be broadcasting the
                first ever pictures next month from Ali Pali.

HOWARD:         Well they should be spending our radio licence
                money on making decent programmes, not on
                all this new rubbish.

DOREEN:         We must keep up with the times sir.

KATHERINE:      What does it do?

| | |
|---|---|
| DOREEN: | Well, they send the signal and it appears on the screen. |
| ALICE: | What does? |
| DOREEN: | The picture. A moving picture, like at the cinema, only in your house. |
| BEA: | Get away? |
| TILLY: | You'd have a job seeing Shirley Temple on that. |
| KATHERINE: | You mean, we could have films, in our homes? |
| DOREEN: | Not films. Programmes, like on the wireless. |
| BEA: | Go on then, show us one. |
| DOREEN: | Well I can't at the moment. |
| ALICE: | Why? |
| DOREEN: | Because they haven't started broadcasting yet. |
| HOWARD: | Oh it's all a con, it's just a glorified fish bowl. |
| TILLY: | Let's have a listen instead then. |
| DOREEN: | You have to have the sound and vision together, that's how it's sent. |
| HOWARD: | So you can't listen in to ordinary radio programmes? |
| DOREEN: | No. |
| BEA: | I can't see you selling many of them. I'd sooner watch a light bulb, with the gramophone on, at least you can still do the ironing. |

*HOWARD stays to talk to DOREEN as the others walk away.*

TILLY:        (*Tittering to Bea*)  If they'd have thought there was any future in that why would they have just opened a new film studio at Pinewood?

BEA:        Yeah.  As if people would rather sit at home alone with their 'television', when they can go to the picture house instead?

*DOT and MARY enter.*

KATHERINE:    That's right, I can't wait to get out.  Can you imagine if you had all this stuff in your house? You wouldn't have to go anywhere; I bet you'd never even see the neighbours.

TILLY:        You should get out more, it suits you.

KATHERINE:    He doesn't like it.  Besides all our money's gone on the house.

BEA:        So, get a job yourself:  earn a bit of your own money.  They're always looking for people where we are.

KATHERINE:    At the works?

BEA:        Yeah, it's nice earning your own tush; you don't have to tell anyone exactly how much your getting for a start.

TILLY:        Hey, that's what I need:  An electric exercise belt.  Forget gymnastics, I could do this while I read my magazines.

*They start to look at the appliances.*

KNOTCHEL:    It's Alice isn't it?

ALICE:        Yes, Lady Knotchel.  I'm terribly sorry about my father's behaviour last month…

KNOTCHEL:    Don't mention it dear.  It's that poor young man I feel sorry for.

WOOLWARD:  And his family, how terrible.

TULCHAN: People have no sense when they get behind a wheel, that's the trouble. They've had to put traffic signals up in London, with red and green lights, just to tell drivers to stop.

KNOTCHEL: How is your father?

ALICE: Not good I'm afraid. He's convinced the Grim Reaper's on his way for him. There's nothing to distract him from it. Especially now he's nothing else to think of.

KNOTCHEL: Do you think a job would take his mind off it?

ALICE: Maybe, but there's no farm work around here anymore; and I'd want him somewhere I could keep an eye on him.

*As they continue to talk IRIS enters and walks excitedly over to TILLY and the others.*

IRIS: I'm going to fly!

BEA: What?

IRIS: I'm going to be a pilot; I've just been talking to Alan Cobham.

BEA: Who's Alan Cobham?

IRIS: 'Alan Cobham's Flying Circus'

TILLY: Awe Iris, it's hardly Amelia Earhart; all that wing walking and acrobatics?

IRIS: Flying is flying.

TILLY: I bet he won't let you anywhere near the controls.

IRIS: Once I know the basics I'll quit and look for a sponsor.

*The SHANKS GANG mooch back in.*

KNOTCHEL: (*To ALICE*) Do you think gardening is beneath your father?

- 88 -

ALICE:      He hasn't even got a garden where he is at the moment.

KNOTCHEL:   But I have.

JOE:        (*To Grace, referring to Knotchel*)   Look at her, rubbing our noses in it.

FLO:        She can afford to.

JOE:        Just 'cos she's got a bit of tush, don't make her any better than us.

KID:        Means she can buy two cars though.

JOE:        My old man fought in the war for the likes of her.

GRACE:      So did mine, for all of us.

JOE:        And where were all these Lords and Ladies? Sitting at home supping tea with their friends, while their old man ordered another few thousand over the top?   (*Beat*)   Here, where's her car?

FLO:        Why?

JOE:        I'm sure I remember seeing the tyres were flat?

*JOE takes out a knife, then exits, followed by GRACE and CHARLIE.   Meanwhile SHANKS has made his way over to HOWARD.*

SHANKS:     You're the bloke who's bought up Little Danson ain't you?

HOWARD:     Yes, what about it?

SHANKS:     Making it into a dance hall I hear?

HOWARD:     That's right.

SHANKS:     Perhaps I should introduce you to my gang.

HOWARD:      What those two?

SHANKS:      No, no there's more of us than that.   The others are erm, they're…   Anyway, you insured?

HOWARD:      What?

SHANKS:      Insured, you know?   There's a lot of vandalism around here at the moment, would be a shame if something happened to your dance hall wouldn't it?

HOWARD:      How'd you mean?

SHANKS:      Well, you know, accident's happen.

HOWARD:      Are you threatening me, you little shit?

*They continue arguing as…*

KATHERINE:   Iris, have you any idea how dangerous flying is?

IRIS:        Of course.

BEA:         Well I say 'well done'.

IRIS:        It's something I've always wanted to do.

KATHERINE:   That's no reason to throw your life away! Planes are death traps.   I thought you of all people would appreciate that.

IRIS:        If you're going to go, you're going to go; so you might as well enjoy yourself.   If nothing else, Bertie's crash taught me that.

DOT:         How dare you speak like that!

IRIS:        What?

DOT:         As if his death was just a 'lesson' for you.

IRIS:        I wasn't saying…

MARY:        She's a bit upset still.

DOT:            If he hadn't been trying to impress you he'd
                still be here today.

IRIS:           You can't blame me for his accident?

DOT:            You left him to die!

IRIS:           I did everything I could!  He was...

DOT:            We had lives before you lot came you know?
                The world didn't end at the top of Shooters
                Hill.  Why don't you go home, the lot of you?

*DOT storms off, followed by MARY.  IRIS stands firm,
before bursting into tears.  She is aided off by BEA.*

TILLY:          What was all that about?

KATHERINE:      It's about how we deal with things that are out
                of our control.

*HOWARD now has SHANKS by the throat.*

DOREEN:         Please, be careful of the televisions.  Let's not
                have violence on our televisions, please.

SHANKS:         I don't care if you hit me, it won't make any
                difference.

HOWARD:         It'll make me feel a whole lot better.

SHANKS:         You can't be there twenty four hours a day.

HOWARD:         Eh?

SHANKS:         Petty crime.  The coppers ain't interested.

HOWARD:         What do you mean?

SHANKS:         It's a lot of trouble; unnecessary trouble.
                Broken windows take time to fix -  if you've
                got the time then smack me one now.

*HOWARD releases him.*

SHANKS: Pennies, that's all we're asking. Look at the kids around here - terrible nuisance.

*ALICE comes over to them, pleased.*

SHANKS: (*As he walks away*) Think about it, eh?

*SHANKS straightens his collar and indicates to FLO and the KID it is time to leave. They follow him out.*

ALICE: Who was that?

HOWARD: No one, just some kid offering to clean the windows.

ALICE: He's keen, they haven't laid the foundations yet, have they?

HOWARD: No.

ALICE: (*Pleased*) I've got my father a job.

HOWARD: What sort of job?

ALICE: Working for Lady Knotchel, as a gardener.

HOWARD: Does he want to be a gardener?

ALICE: We said we'll see how he gets on.

*ANNE, AGNES and EDD walk in.*

HOWARD: Don't look now, it's the ugly sisters.

TILLY: (*To Katherine*) Why are you so concerned about Iris being a pilot?

KATHERINE: Because it's a dangerous profession.

TILLY: How do you know?

KATHERINE: Because my husband was a pilot.

TILLY: Bomullock?

KATHERINE: Not him.

TILLY:         You've been married before?

KATHERINE:   I still am.

TILLY:         I know that, I mean to someone else?

KATHERINE:   No.  I'm not married to him.

TILLY:         You're not married to old Bomullock!?
               You're a dark horse.

KATHERINE:   He's my brother-in-law.

TILLY:         You ran away with your brother-in-law!!?
               Blimey, if he was the nice one, I'd hate to see
               the one you married.

KATHERINE:   Tilly, you must promise me you won't breath a
               word of this to anyone?

TILLY:         Alright.

KATHERINE:   Jack, my husband, was killed in a plane crash
               during the war.  His plane burst into flames,
               they're far too flimsy...  Anyway a few weeks
               after he died we received a cheque.  It was a
               pension, but not a widow's pension, so I
               thought he was still alive.  But he never came
               home.  A couple of days later Jack's brother
               said we should collect the money, so we had it
               for when he came back.  I didn't think it
               would matter, because he'd be home soon and
               we needed to eat, there wasn't any work.  But
               of course it was a mistake, he never did come
               home.  Only by then we'd collected too much
               money.  His brother said it would be best if we
               kept quiet:  no-one need ever know he was
               forging Jack's signature.  Trouble is, we saw
               less and less of the money.  The old lady was
               so upset at losing one of her sons, she daren't
               do anything to upset the other one.  And that's
               how it's gone on – lie after lie.  I can't sleep at
               night sometimes.

TILLY:         Why don't you leave him, get away?

KATHERINE: Because he'll tell the police, tell them I knew that Jack was dead all this time. If I was going to leave I'd have to get right away, but I don't see any of that money. I can only just about buy us food with what he gives me.

TILLY: You can't be a prisoner in your own house.

KATHERINE: Promise me you won't tell a soul? If he finds out I've told anyone…

*ALICE walks over to ANNE.*

ALICE: Hello Anne.

EDD: Hey, now come on, I don't want any trouble.

ALICE: Can't I speak to my own sister?

ANNE: What do you want Alice?

ALICE: Would you come and visit Pa?

ANNE: He doesn't want to see me.

ALICE: He doesn't want to see me either, but you're still his daughter.

EDD: Look love, she doesn't want to see the old git. Last time he came up to our house he started shouting and screaming…

HOWARD: I think this is a family matter, don't you?

EDD: And who are you? That's my wife she's talking to.

HOWARD: All I'm saying is…

ANNE: It's all right Eddy, I'm not intimidated by my little sister.

*She glances at AGNES, who turns her back on ALICE and walks off to look at another part of the display. EDD sizes up the situation, then decides to back down.*

EDD:            (*To Anne*)  Don't you let her talk you out of
                any assets my darling.

*He walks over to AGNES, HOWARD walks over to the
IRON LADY.*

ANNE:           Well?

ALICE:          I just think, if you could come and see him, it
                might help.  He might recognise you.

TILLY:          (*To Katherine*)  So, to get away, you need
                money – right?

KATHERINE:      And there's none to spare.

TILLY:          Unless you had a job?

KATHERINE:      He'll never agree to that.

TILLY:          Then don't tell him.  He's out all day, and she
                won't know where you are.

KATHERINE:      But I'd come home filthy, like you do.

TILLY:          Then get a job in the canteen.  It's only across
                the road, you'd be finished by four.

KATHERINE:      I couldn't.

TILLY:          Don't know what that word means.  You
                could keep every penny you earned.  In six
                months you'd have enough to hop on a boat at
                Erith and you'd be away.

KATHERINE:      Six months?

TILLY:          Try it for a week or so, what have you got to
                lose?

ANNE:           (*To ALICE*)  If he didn't want us to have the
                farm, perhaps he shouldn't have given it to us
                so readily.  I was prepared to work my time.

ALICE:          So why didn't you?

- 95 -

ANNE:           Because I didn't have to.   He was so annoyed
                with you, he couldn't give it away fast enough.
                Why do you always make things so difficult
                for yourself Alice?   Here.

ALICE:          What are you doing?

ANNE:           Here's a few pounds for you.

ALICE:          I don't want your money.

ANNE:           Take it.

ALICE:          I don't want it, I'm not your husband.

ANNE:           And just what do you mean by that?

ALICE:          Ask your kitchen skivvy.

*ALICE exits abruptly.   EDD and AGNES watch her go.
EDD removes his arm from around AGNES' waist
quickly and smiles at ANNE.*

### Autocratic Outrage (reprise)

You think it gives you authority,
To put down the majority,
When all of us can quite plainly see,
That you're no better than him or me.

It's all wrong,
Stops you getting on,
It's time to refuse,
The birth right blues,
And an undemocratic, systematic,
                        autocratic  outrage.
It's an outrage.

## SCENE TWELVE: Lady Knotchel's Living Room – August 1936

*LADY KNOTCHEL sits with LADY WOOLWARD and LADY TULCHAN.*

KNOTCHEL: …I saw Inspector Levett and said to him, 'just what do you propose to do about all this youth crime?'

WOOLWARD: And what did he say to that?

KNOTCHEL: 'We can't keep an eye on every spotty Herbert, it's the parent's who should be doing that job'.

TULCHAN: Oh, how ridiculous.

WOOLWARD: I don't know what the country's coming to, look at that fellow who took a pot shot at the King!

TULCHAN: Places like that children's home act as a training ground.

KNOTCHEL: It's the Londoners, they don't care you see, they don't have any respect for their own surroundings.

TULCHAN: At least when the old estates survived they where run by men with a social conscience: that's what's missing today. Perhaps some of them were railway men, of little breeding, but they looked after people as well as any Lord.

WOOLWARD: Pretty soon Lady Limeric will be the only aristocrat left – no one else will want to stay.

TULCHAN: Yes, but what a way to live? The local authority owning your family house? Disgraceful.

WOOLWARD: Hall Place represents one of the last decent sizeable houses left.

TULCHAN: And who knows what plans they have for that? They could turn it into a pub, for all we know.

WOOLWARD: Edward had better have his coronation soon, there'll be no space left to erect a coronation bonfire.

*MARY enters.*

MARY: Miss Hurst's here to see you ma'am.

KNOTCHEL: Thank you. Show her in would you?

TULCHAN: I don't know how you've stayed on as long as you have.

*KNOTCHEL places her finger to her lips.*
*MARY exits.*

WOOLWARD: Is this 'Alice' the old man's daughter?

KNOTCHEL: Yes.

TULCHAN: I do think it's marvellous the way you've helped him out.

WOOLWARD: It's such a shame that all his hard work will have been for nothing now.

*ALICE enters with MARY.*

KNOTCHEL: Thank you for coming at such short notice.

ALICE: Not at all Lady Knotchel, is it about my father?

KNOTCHEL: Yes, yes it is. Thank you Mary, that will be all.

*MARY exits.*

ALICE: Oh I am sorry. What's he done now? He seemed to be getting on so well.

KNOTCHEL: Oh nothing, nothing. On the contrary he's been getting on very well here.

ALICE: Thank heavens for that. It really has given him a new lease of life, especially as he's been able to stay in the gardener's cottage. It's been a weight off my mind as well, to tell you the truth.

KNOTCHEL: Yes.

WOOLWARD: Good gardeners are hard to find, I'm sure he could find work anywhere now.

TULCHAN: Especially with a good reference from Lady Knotchel.

ALICE: Yes, I suppose he could. But he wouldn't want to work anywhere else, he's settled here.

KNOTCHEL: Yes…, that may be so, but circumstances being what they are…

ALICE: Which circumstances?

KNOTCHEL: I'm sure, once he's settled in, one place will be much the same as another.

WOOLWARD: They're bound to need people at the park?

TULCHAN: And the council rent's are so reasonable.

ALICE: I thought his gardening duties covered any rent?

KNOTCHEL: I'm not charging him rent.

ALICE: Then you're renting the cottage to someone else?

TULCHAN: I'm sure even he has noticed a change in situation, regarding the area.

WOOLWARD: We were just discussing how things have altered around here.

ALICE: Of course but…

KNOTCHEL: I'm afraid I have sold the house.

ALICE: This house?

KNOTCHEL: The time has come to move on.

ALICE: But it's your family home?

KNOTCHEL: Once; but a hundred yards from the front gates and I couldn't tell you where I was these days.

TULCHAN: I lose my bearings once I'm over Shooters Hill, and I've only been gone five years.

ALICE: Where will you go?

KNOTCHEL: For now I have the flat in London.

ALICE: A flat? With no grounds, no garden?

KNOTCHEL: I know, it will be a terrible shock to the system.

ALICE: Then what will he have to do?

TULCHAN: My dear, she wasn't offering to take your father with her.

WOOLWARD: As I said, he'll have no trouble getting work.

TULCHAN: People will always need their gardens dug.

ALICE: He's not a gardener!

KNOTCHEL: I know dear... Well, there it is. I thought perhaps the news would be best coming from you?

ALICE: Me? Why should I do your dirty work for you?

KNOTCHEL: I beg your pardon?

ALICE: If you want to tell him, you can tell him yourself.

*ALICE walks over to the window.*

ALICE: Pa! Pa!! (*No response*) Mr. Hurst!

HURST: (*Off*) Yes ma'am, coming ma'am.

KNOTCHEL:    Alice, there really is no need…

ALICE:    Oh yes there is.

KNOTCHEL:    Why make things harder than they are?

ALICE:    You don't know what hardship is.

KNOTCHEL:    Do you think this is what I want: to leave my home?  The place I knew has been washed away under a tide of tarmac.  Do you think I have made this decision lightly?

ALICE:    At least you've got a choice.

*HURST enters.*

HURST:    I've planted out the seeds in the herb garden and I'm working on the chrysanth's now. There's a nest of ants up at the back there'll need sorting out, but I'll leave that 'til this afternoon.

KNOTCHEL:    Don't worry about that now.

HURST:    You can't leave it, biters they are.  You'll never be able to sit up there, and it's the best part of the garden…

ALICE:    No-one'll be sitting up there pa.

HURST:    Stop calling me that will you!  Sorry your ladyship, these girls they, they like to tease an old man, they…

KNOTCHEL:    I'm sorry to have to tell you this, but…

HURST:    (*Suddenly stone faced*)  He's been?  He's been here hasn't he?

WOOLWARD:    Who?

ALICE:    He hasn't been here.

HURST:    Don't lie to me!

- 101 -

KNOTCHEL:    It's alright, no-one's come for you.

HURST:    (*Very distressed*) I knew he'd find me, I knew it. You can't cheat him, you can't. I got to get away, take me self out of here.

ALICE:    He hasn't come for you.

HURST:    Why can't he leave me alone. Why can't you leave me be!!

TULCHAN:    What's he going on about?

HURST:    (*To Alice*) You, you must have lead him to me! He'll take us all, he'll take us all. Why did you tell him where I was? Why? Pack my things, that's what I'll do. No. No time, no time. He's here already, I can sense it, he'll be there at the cottage. Can't go back there, can't go back there. Must get to the farm house. Back to the farm, Bess, she'll know what to do. That's it Bess, she'll know.

ALICE:    She's gone pa. Mum's gone.

HURST:    Oh God, oh God, he's got her. He's got her and now he's come for me. He's taken them all. Oh Alice, Alice...

ALICE:    Yes.

HURST:    Get away from me! Whoever you are. I knew he'd find me. I knew it. He's taken them and now he wants me. Where can I go, where can I go? He'll know, he'll know, wherever. You can't hide from him, he's been watching, waiting, I know it. Can't go back, can't go back to the cottage, not there, he'll know, he's waiting. Can't go there. Can't go back to the farm house. He thinks I did it, that's why he wants me. He thinks I did it, that's why. Thinks I killed them but I didn't, I didn't do it. Or maybe I did, maybe I did? Dear sweet Bess, dear sweet Alice? Maybe I did? I can't... How, how? I can't even remember. He's...

ALICE:          Stop it, stop it!

HURST:         Please, please don't let him take me. I'm
sorry for what I did, I didn't mean to burn
them. I didn't know I'd done it. Please, you
have to believe me. I can't go back there,
he'll find me. He'll come for me. I didn't
mean to do it. He knows I'm here. Don't let
him take me, don't let him take me!

*HURST collapses, sobbing hysterically. ALICE tries to
comfort him while the others sit awkwardly, unsure of
what to do.*

### Step Up (reprise)

Come on, step up and be entertained,
Kick the blues from your shoes and be happy
again,
Take your mind off the times and sing a
cheerful refrain,
Come on, step up and be entertained.

Why think you're a loser with a life that's
mundane,
If a dice would be nice to spin you out of your
chains,
Let the board game un-bore you, be a winner
again,
Come on, step up and be entertained.

Come on, step up and be entertained,
Kick the blues from your shoes and be happy
again,
Take your mind off the times and sing a
cheerful refrain,
Come on, step up and be entertained.

## SCENE THIRTEEN:   The Kitchen, Bomullock's House – October 1936

*The cramped kitchen of their terraced house. TILLY, LUCY, KATHERINE, BEA, IRIS and MARY sit around a Monopoly board at a small table.*

KATHERINE:    What's it called again?

TILLY:    Monopoly.

BEA:    And what's the idea?

TILLY:    You go around the board buying up land, and then you build houses and charge people rent.

LUCY:    Well that doesn't sound like a very interesting game to me.

TILLY:    It's all the rage in America, believe me. Right, has everybody got their money?

KATHERINE:    Oh, that reminds me.

TILLY:    Come back, we haven't started yet.  OK Lucy, you go first.

LUCY:    Three.

TILLY:    Whitechapel Road, sixty pounds.

LUCY:    Is that all?

BEA:    If you've seen Whitechapel Road lately you'd ask for a discount.

TILLY:    Come on, sixty pounds.   Right, and here's your card.

KATHERINE:    (*Placing a tin on the table*)   There.

TILLY:    (*Looking in the box*)   Blimey Kath, we don't need real money to play this you know?

KATHERINE:    That's my first three months wages from Vickers.  By December I'll have enough to get out of here.

IRIS:           Are you really going?

KATHERINE:   I've made up my mind.

LUCY:           Where are you going?

TILLY:          Never you mind young lady.   And I don't
                want you to breath a word, or else I'll be
                putting those bees under your pillow.

LUCY:           I can keep a secret you know?

IRIS:           Five.   Two hundred quid for a manky old
                station!

TILLY:          Kings Cross?   It's a big station.

IRIS:           Give us it here then.

BEA:            Your old man still got the bees then?

LUCY:           Yes.

TILLY:          It's a bit of an obsession at the moment, he's
                planning on taking them to the South London
                Exhibition at The Crystal Palace.

IRIS:           For a day out?

BEA:            Four.

TILLY:          No, to the show.

BEA:            'Income tax'?

LUCY:           Two hundred pounds to the bank please.   I'm
                going to see Gracie Fields at the Palace.

TILLY:          You and thirty thousand others.

LUCY:           Out of the whole country.

BEA:            That's good Luce.

TILLY:          It's a concert for the King's coronation.

Darren Rapier

BEA:            Here.  Do they still have that talent show at the Palace?

TILLY:          I think so, yeah.

KATHERINE:   'Chance'.  What's that?

TILLY:          Oh, you need one of these.

KATHERINE:   'Get out of jail free'.

TILLY:          You might need that later.

BEA:            I think we should enter it.  You never know who's at these things.

IRIS:           I thought you wanted to be a broadcaster?

MARY:          Kings Cross.  Can I buy it as well?

TILLY:          No, Iris has already got it.  Hang on a minute... oh yeah, you owe her twenty-five pounds.

MARY:          Why?

TILLY:          Because you landed on her station.

MARY:          Well that's not fair.

TILLY:          It is, she bought it.  You can buy something later on.

MARY:          Typical.  Someone gets there first, so we have to do what they say.

TILLY:          Pay up and don't be so bitter.  You found another job didn't you?

MARY:          I hate shop work.

BEA:            What's the difference?  You're still serving people.

MARY:          I've gone right off chocolate.

TILLY:      My turn. 'Chance'. 'You have won second prize in a beauty contest, collect ten pounds'. Maybe we should enter that talent contest, eh Bea?

BEA:      We'd need to practice, of course. I've got some Gloria Duvall records we could listen to.

TILLY:      Oh don't talk to me about Gloria Duvall - Howard's trying to book her for the opening night at the ballroom.

BEA:      'The' Gloria Duvall?

TILLY:      Yes, but she's being a right pain. She wants to stay at the Lamorbey Park Hotel, no where else, all expenses paid of course...

BEA:      Wouldn't you like to be like that?

TILLY:      I wouldn't be like that.

BEA:      She got discovered at a talent show.

KATHERINE:   Did she?

TILLY:      Alright, I'll give it a go.

BEA:      'Marry me, and I'll never look at another horse'.

TILLY:      Groucho Marx, Day at the Races.

IRIS:      Will you two stop doing that?

LUCY:      Chance.

KATHERINE:   I own that one.

TILLY:      You can't buy a 'chance' Katherine. There you go kid.

LUCY:      'Speeding fine, fifteen pounds'.

*MOTHER BOMULLOCK enters.*

M BOMULLOCK:   What's going on?

KATHERINE:   (*Removing her tin from the table*)   We're just playing a new board game.

M BOMULLOCK:   Does he know?

TILLY:   It's only a game.

M BOMULLOCK:   You best be finishing up now.

LUCY:   We've only just started.

M BOMULLOCK:   Put the kettle on Katherine, he'll be home soon.

*MOTHER BOMULLOCK exits.*

TILLY:   (*Pretending to read a Chance card*)   'You are sold as a suburban slave to a mother and son'.

MARY:   Shh Tilly, she'll hear you.

TILLY:   Oh let her hear, the old battle axe.   Your turn Iris.

IRIS:   I'm in Jail.

TILLY:   Just visiting, here.   You have to land over there to go to jail, or pick up a card that sends you there.

BEA:   'Angel Islington', I'll buy that.

MARY:   Is that girl still living with you Till?

TILLY:   No, she's gone to stay with her father:   he's in a bad way, they've got lodgings down near the works.   Howard's still seeing her mind.

KATHERINE:   'Electric Company', that should be worth a few bob.

MARY:   I think he'd had some sort of a break down. He used to scare me with all his talk of ghosts coming to take him away.

TILLY:  He's lost everything he ever had, poor sod.

MARY:  'Pentonville Road'.  Can I have one of those little houses as well?

TILLY:  Not yet.  You have to wait until you've got all the streets in that set.

LUCY:  This is boring.

TILLY:  That's one hundred and twenty pounds please.

BEA:  Have you seen those new handbags in Hides? They've got a special zipper pocket for your gas mask.

TILLY:  'Just visiting', with you Iris.

MARY:  I haven't been given a gas mask yet.

TILLY:  We won't need 'em.  I'm going to get a sequinned nozzle for mine, have you seen them?

IRIS:  I wouldn't be so sure we won't need them, the Italian's have been using mustard gas in Abyssinia.

TILLY:  Well that ain't here is it?

MARY:  I don't want to be the only one without, do I?

LUCY:  Pall Mall.

TILLY:  That's a hundred and forty pounds to you, young lady.

*BOMULLOCK enters.*

BOMULLOCK:  What do you lot think you're doing in here?

KATHERINE:  I didn't hear you come in.

BOMULLOCK:  I won't have gambling in my house.

TILLY:  It's not gambling, it's play money.

*BOMULLOCK tips up the board.*

LUCY:           Hey, we were playing that!

BOMULLOCK:  Take it elsewhere.

*Sheepishly the women gather up the pieces and exit.*

TILLY:          See you later Katherine.

*KATHERINE stands for a moment, she notices her money tin has been left on the table.*

BOMULLOCK:  Go and clean my boots.  I'll make my own tea.

*KATHERINE exits swiftly, collecting her tin on the way.*

BOMULLOCK:  Just a minute.

*She stops dead.*

BOMULLOCK:  You can take my coat as well.

*He hands her the coat and she exits swiftly. As BOMULLOCK makes his tea MOTHER BOMULLOCK enters.*

M BOMULLOCK:  Son?

BOMULLOCK:  What is it?

M BOMULLOCK:  Do you have to be so hard on her?

BOMULLOCK:  Look after her, don't I?

M BOMULLOCK:  I know but…

BOMULLOCK:  Treat 'em mean and keep 'em keen.

M BOMULLOCK:  I thought I saw someone again today, at the window.

BOMULLOCK:  Probably one of those Jarrow marchers, after a free meal, littering up the streets.  Baldwin had the right idea: tell them to bugger off back home.

M BOMULLOCK: I couldn't see anyone when I went outside.

BOMULLOCK: (*Mocking*) So you think it's the spirit of Jack, checking up on us?

M BOMULLOCK: You can't keep her cooped up all the time...

BOMULLOCK: If she's supposed to be my wife then I can do what I like, can't I?

M BOMULLOCK: Yes but...

BOMULLOCK: I didn't choose to look after her. It wasn't me who promised to love, honour and all the rest of it. That was Jack. He chose to go off and leave her, no-one forced him to be a pilot. He could have worked on the ships like the rest of us, but oh no, not Jack. And if it wasn't for me, could she draw his pension? No: I'm forced to lie for her.

M BOMULLOCK: But you earn your own money, down at Erith now.

BOMULLOCK: That's my money, nothing to do with you or her. Jack's money keeps you and that's all you need.

M BOMULLOCK: I'm not sure we should be doing this.

BOMULLOCK: And how can we stop now? Tell them it was all a mistake, that Jack died in 1918? What do you think they'll say to that? 'Oh don't worry, keep the money'. They'd want it back, all of it. Where are we going to be then eh? Back in the gutter, that's where.

M BOMULLOCK: Jack managed to...

BOMULLOCK: Jack, Jack? I'm fed up with hearing about Jack. He's dead mother and that's that. You're as bad as that loopy farmer.

### Brick by Brick (Reprise)

Brick by brick,
Brick by brick,
Brick by brick…

Behind closed doors,
The secrets locked in,
Hidden from daylight,
But plans are scored to change things.

Brick by brick,
Brick by brick,
Brick by brick…

## SCENE FOURTEEN:   Tench's Builders Office – Late October 1936

*TENCH, slightly puzzled, sits behind his desk.   In front of him are a set of blueprints for an estate.   Facing him on the other side of the desk are ANNE and AGNES.*

| | |
|---|---|
| TENCH: | …these plans are no use to me, I have my own architects and surveyors.   Besides, there's far too many houses on each acre. |
| ANNE: | Then feel free to dispose of them as you wish Mr. Tench. |
| TENCH: | But it must have cost you money, to have such detailed plans drawn up? |
| AGNES: | There's more to life than money. |
| ANNE: | We want the land developed by a local builder, like yourself, not some big company; or someone who's simply out to make a fast profit. |
| TENCH: | Then why not take it to Hawkins, or Bowyer? |
| ANNE: | Because we've come to you first. |
| TENCH: | You know I can get over six hundred pounds for a completed house?   And twenty's the maximum I can offer you per plot. |
| AGNES: | That's fine. |
| TENCH: | I've got to be competitive you see, empty houses are no good to anyone. |
| ANNE: | It's fine. |

*Beat.*

| | |
|---|---|
| TENCH: | I remember strawberry picking at your father's farm, when I was a lad.   We'd go early in the season, to get the best one's before the Londoners arrived. |

ANNE:      That's when we grew market crops and clover; lucerne and tares for the horses at Courage's, in Southwark. We could make the farm pay then.

AGNES:     I used to ride up with the carter sometimes; he'd have so many treats the horse'd have to find its own way home.

TENCH:     Aye, they haven't made a car yet that can do that. How is Mr Hurst, I'd heard he was unwell.

ANNE:      He's fine.

TENCH:     You know, if you sold the farm off for self-build plots - like they have at Blackfen - you could probably get a bit more? It would take longer, but five or six pounds per plot would make a huge difference on the selling price.

ANNE:      We want to sell it in one go, Mr. Tench.

TENCH:     Well, all the paperwork seems to be in order so…

*TENCH takes his cheque book and writes the cheque.*

TENCH:     What will you do with your money ladies?

AGNES:     We're moving away.

ANNE:      Yes, we don't really like the area anymore.

TENCH:     Anywhere nice?

*He hands over the cheque, in return for the deeds.*

AGNES:     Germany.

TENCH:     Oh?

ANNE:      We went there on holiday in '32. It's a beautiful country.

TENCH:     You don't think things have changed a bit since then?

- 114 -

AGNES: You can't believe all the propaganda can you?

ANNE: Everything changes Mr. Tench.

*Suddenly EDD bursts in.*

EDD: What's going on?

AGNES: You're too late, the farm belongs to Mr. Tench now.

EDD: What!

ANNE: Oh and the divorce papers are in the post.

EDD: It ain't yours to sell, we're still married.

ANNE: Yes it is, my father made sure of that in the original papers.

EDD: (*To Anne*)  What's she been filling your head with?  It ain't true, whatever it is.

AGNES: Ohh!

EDD: She's lying...  Jealousy, that's what it is.

ANNE: Blood is thicker than water Eddy, but not as thick as you.

EDD: Come on, we can make a fresh start.  We can just develop our half, forget her.

AGNES: How dare you!

EDD: She seduced me love, and now she's trying to ruin everything.

ANNE: You are unbelievable.

EDD: That's my land!

TENCH: I think you'll find it's mine now.

EDD: You crook!

- 115 -

TENCH:       I'll have you know, I've been building houses
             in round here for the past twenty years; I
             worked for Thomas Knight.  In those days you
             had to be a craftsman, not some 'do-it-
             yourself', 'make it up as you go along'
             cowboy.

EDD:         I have as much right to build houses as the next
             man.

AGNES:       Not on that land you don't.

EDD:         Damn it Anne, almost everything else has been
             bought up!  I'll be building houses out on the
             marshes at this rate.

ANNE:        That really is all you care about isn't it?  Not
             me, not her, just how many houses you can fit
             into the smallest space possible?  And what
             about after you'd got what you wanted from
             us, eh?  What then?  On to the next project?
             On to the next gullible country bumpkin?  I
             should have listened to my father when I had
             the chance.  Come on Agnes, I don't like the
             taste of the air 'round here any more.

*ANNE and AGNES exit.  EDD hesitates for a moment..*

EDD:         Well you ain't having my plans.

*He snatches up the plans and exits.*
*TENCH shakes his head in dismay.*


### Boom (reprise)

(*Slow*)   One November night,
           At it's South London sight,
           Crystal Palace caught light,
           And flames soon spread.

           As the iron frame glowed,
           Then buckled and bowed,
           Things began to explode,
           And the glass went Boom!

Boom, boom, boom,
Boom, boom, boom,
Boom, the glass went boom!

Boom, boom, boom,
Boom, boom, boom,
Boom, boom, boom, boom, Boom!

### SCENE FIFTEEN:   The Top of Shooters Hill – 9:00pm, November 30th, 1936

*From the crest of the hill the blaze of the Crystal Palace can be seen.  The glass palace, covering four times the ground area of St. Peter's in Rome, lights up the sky as the iron and glass structure burns white hot.  There are a lot of people already there as TILLY, LUCY, BEA, IRIS, HOWARD and ALICE reach the top.  In front of them is 1930's London, behind the changed face of North West Kent.*

| | |
|---|---|
| LUCY: | Oh my God, look at it. |
| TILLY: | Don't blaspheme Lucy… (*She sees the blaze*) Jesus Christ! |
| HOWARD: | Looks like the Kings got his coronation bonfire alright. |
| ALICE: | The whole place must have gone up? |
| IRIS: | I'd better get back to the hospital. |
| BEA: | What's the point, no-one's going to get through that traffic. |
| HOWARD: | Anyway there's a good few hospitals between here and Sydenham. |
| IRIS: | Not with the best plastic surgery department in the world. |
| TILLY: | How can all that glass and iron burn? |
| IRIS: | Anything'll burn, if it gets hot enough. |
| MAY: | Alright Tilly? |
| TILLY: | How long have you lot been up here? |
| GINNY: | Since about six, and there were already people here then. |
| MAY: | They said, on the wireless, it might be arson. |
| BEA: | Why? |

ALICE:    Who would want to burn down the Crystal
          Palace?  It's the biggest landmark in South
          East London.

IRIS:     Exactly.  Think about it:  with the moon light
          reflecting in all that glass, there'd be no
          problem working out where you are from the
          air.

LUCY:     So?

IRIS:     Bomber planes.  You can black out the whole
          of London, but you can't black out the moon.

ALICE:    That's true.  I can remember the Zeppelin
          bombers, following the Thames, like silver
          giants.

IRIS:     The planes can fly higher than the Zeppelins
          ever could.  And with a landmark like that,
          they could pin point exactly where they were,
          in relation to the river.

HOWARD:   Hitler would never send planes over here.

IRIS:     I wouldn't be so sure.  One day the whole of
          London could look like that.

TILLY:    Don't say that Iris, you're frightening Lucy.

LUCY:     How am I going to see Gracie Fields now?

TILLY:    Don't worry Lucy, they'll find somewhere
          else.

BEA:      As the Palace?

HOWARD:   They must have every fire engine in London
          there.

MAY:      And most of Kent I'd imagine.

BEA:      What about all the shows, all the concerts
          booked up for Christmas?

| | |
|---|---|
| TILLY: | I'm sure they'll put some temporary building up, until they can re-build it. |
| BEA: | I hope so; don't want all our practice going to waste. |
| GINNY: | What was that? |
| HOWARD: | Looked like an explosion. |
| MAY: | It must be like Hell's kitchen up there. |

*The TELLER and the GYPSY have appeared behind the crowd.*

| | |
|---|---|
| TELLER: | The ghost of the last war, will return to haunt us once more! |
| HOWARD: | Will you stop doing that! |
| GYPSY: | She's had another vision. |
| MAY: | She'll have a kick up the arse in a minute. |
| TELLER: | The flames, the flames. |
| TILLY: | Don't worry Lucy. |
| HOWARD: | How much will it cost for you to keep your mouth shut? |
| TELLER: | Flames from the sky. |
| GINNY: | She's off her nut. |
| IRIS: | Clear off will you, we don't want your doom and gloom around here. |
| BEA: | Yeah, we've come up here to watch the Palace burning. |
| HOWARD: | Here, there's no need to show this on those televisions, eh? You can see it all over London as it is. |
| BEA: | Look at those planes Iris. |

IRIS:   They must be from Croydon, the pictures'll be worth a fortune.

GINNY:   My old man always said the place was a monstrosity.

*TILLY has turned to wrap LUCY up, she looks over the hill facing south.*

TILLY:   Woah, look at that.

ALICE:   What?

TILLY:   Look at all the lights.

BEA:   Kent's changed a bit, since we used to trundle out here in the old charabancs.

HOWARD:   Weetley's housing act must have worked then?

TELLER:   It will get dark, before it gets light.

MAY:   Give it a rest will you?

ALICE:   Acres of electricity.

LUCY:   Can you see our house?

HOWARD:   They all look the same.

GINNY:   Who'd have thought, even at the beginning of this century, that all that land would be full of houses?

ALICE:   Even five years ago you'd have hardly seen a light from here.

MAY:   There's one sure thing: once the city's crept out, it won't come back again. Bexley's just a rock pool now.

BEA:   At least there's countryside beyond that, out in the darkness.

HOWARD:   Yeah, there's loads more countryside.

*RUTH, ISOBEL and SARAH arrive at the top of the hill.*

SARAH:      Have we missed it?

IRIS:       No, it's still burning.

ISOBEL:     Oh good, we brought some sheets to sit on.

BEA:        Great.

RUTH:       Wow.  The whole of London must be at a standstill.

BEA:        Any news on the wireless?

IRIS:       (*To Tilly*)  I'd best get going, just in case.

ALICE:      I'll come with you, I'd better get back to pa.

HOWARD:     See you at Danson tomorrow Alice.

ALICE:      OK.

HOWARD:     The painters start at nine.

*Shanks sidles up.*

SHANKS:     Evening Howard.

HOWARD:     Oh, it's you.

SHANKS:     Don't forget our little deal now, will you?   I mean, we wouldn't want anything nasty to happen on your opening night?

JOE:        Wouldn't want another Crystal Palace.

HOWARD:     I haven't forgotten.

*SHANKS and his gang exit.*

TILLY:      Surely you're not going to pay them?

HOWARD:     What choice do I have?

TILLY:      They're kids Howard.

| | |
|---|---|
| HOWARD: | But they can still ruin the dance hall. |
| TILLY: | Oh come off it. |
| HOWARD: | Till, if there's any trouble that first night people won't come back. |
| TILLY: | So put someone on the door. |
| HOWARD: | I can't afford to have skirmishes outside, what sort of impression will that give? And it's not just that is it? Like he said: any vandalism to people's cars, broken windows – anything. It's not worth it Till, I may as well simply pay them to keep them quiet. |
| TILLY: | And what sort of message is that going to give? They'll just ask for more and more. Go to the police. |
| HOWARD: | And say what? 'I think some kids are trying to ruin my business'? Forget it. I'm up to my neck in this and if it doesn't work we could lose everything, including the house – remember. Our opening night is less than two weeks away – we've booked Gloria bloody Duvall – and it needs to go smoothly; without any dramas, thank you |

*HOWARD exits.*

| | |
|---|---|
| BEA: | (*To Tilly*) What was all that about? |
| TILLY: | Oh, nothing. |
| BEA: | (*Chicago accent*) 'We O'Learys are a strange tribe, but there's strength in us. And what we set out to do, we'll finish'. |
| TILLY: | In Old Chicago? |
| BEA: | (*Same accent*) But who said it sister? |
| TILLY: | Alice Brady? |
| BEA: | Awe, thought I had you there. |

*TILLY suddenly has an idea.*

TILLY:          Bea, how'd you like to put your talent to some practical use?

BEA:          You heard of another singing contest then?

TILLY:          It wasn't singing I had in mind.

### Use That Talent

Look at that Picasso,
He's a paint and portrait king,
And Dali did what he had to do,
Weird landscapes are his thing,
Toulouse-Lautrec said what the heck,
There's money in advertising.

Use it, use that talent,
You should use it, that's for sure.
Use it, use that gift boy,
That's what you got it for.
There ain't no use being the king of swing,
If you won't get on the floor.

Einstein is a fine stein,
He equals M C squared,
And Galileo Galilee,
Watched starry skies instead,
Newton started shooting,
When that apple hit his head.

Use it, use that talent,
You should use it, that's for sure.
Use it, use that gift boy,
That's what you got it for.
There ain't no use being the king of swing,
If you won't get on the floor.

Let's go!

*Instrumental break.*

Use it, use that talent,
You should use it, that's for sure.
Use it, use that gift boy,

That's what you got it for.
There ain't no use being the king of swing,
If you won't get on the floor.

Use it!

## SCENE SIXTEEN:   An Old Warehouse, Erith – Early December 1936

*It is dark.  The lone figure of a woman, standing in silhouette can just me made out.  From her stance it is obvious she is confident and affluent.  In fact she is BEA in a borrowed frock.  The SHANKS GANG enter, nervously, their eyes not yet adjusted to the light.*

BEA:        (*In a perfect hard Chicago accent*)  What took ya so long?

SHANKS:     Who's there?

BEA:        Don't matter who I am kid, it's what I gotta say that's important.

JOE:        Why did you send for us?

BEA:        'Cos I heard that you're the big potatoes 'round here.

CHARLIE:    Big potatoes?

KID:        Is that an insult Shanks?

SHANKS:     Well…

BEA:        It's what we call the 'top dogs' in Chicago.

SHANKS:     (*Impressed*)  Chicago?

BEA:        You got quite a reputation out there.

JOE:        Have we?

BEA:        That's what I'm doing here.

GRACE:      Where are the lights in here, I like to see who I'm talking to.

BEA:        Stay put sweetheart, it's more flattering this way – and believe me, you should know.

FLO:        Ooo, are you going to stand for that?

BEA:           Don't come any closer:  I got a piece, and it ain't shy of barking.

*FLO and GRACE give each other a puzzled look.*

BEA:           You clowns heard of Capone?

SHANKS:     Al Capone?

BEA:           Got it in one Sherlock.  He's my boss, see, and he's looking to… cross the pond.

CHARLIE:    (*Whispering to Kid*)  Have you got any idea what she's on about?

JOE:           (*To Bea*)  I thought he was in prison?

BEA:           Oh?  (*Then confident*)  What of it?

JOE:           How's he going to cross anything if he's banged up?

BEA:           We ain't talking about some dime store cowboy here, this the 'the man'.  You know what I'm saying?

SHANKS:     Yeah, pipe down, this is 'the man' we're talking about.

BEA:           Things are a little hot in the Windy City right now, capiche?  So Al says to me, "You gotta find somewheres else we can start ourselves up".  So I looks around, I do some talking and I come up with…

JOE:           Welling?

BEA:           Sure, who the god damn hell's ever heard of it? And the racket's already set for the man to take over the driving seat.

SHANKS:     Big Al's coming here?

JOE:           Scarface Capone?

BEA:           It's all hush, hush.

JOE:        And he wants us to work for him?

KID:        Do we all get pin striped suits?

FLO:        And long cigarette holders?

BEA:        Not exactly…

CHARLIE:    And those machine guns, like Cagney uses?

SHANKS:     And matchsticks to chew on?

KID:        We've got matchsticks.

BEA:        Shut up already!   Did I just throw a box o' candy into the kindergarten playground?

CHARLIE:    Sorry.

SHANKS:     I knew this was the only way to make it.

BEA:        Make what?

SHANKS:     The big time.

BEA:        You think Scarface would want you dummies working for him?

SHANKS:     But…

BEA:        I came here to give you a warning, not a job.

JOE:        A warning?

BEA:        If you try anything, tell anyone or even take a pin from Hide's haberdashery department, then you'll be dining out on lead.   Understand?

CHARLIE:    So, he doesn't want us to work for him?

BEA:        Al don't like to be crossed, you keep him happy and the undertaker don't get a free world cruise out of the extra business.

JOE:        How do we know you ain't bluffing?

BEA:            Ask the last guy.  But you'll have to be quick,
                high tide's in half an hour.

*Silence.*

BEA:            Now get out o' here, your faces is making me
                nauseous.

*They fall over each other trying to find the door.*
*TILLY comes out of the shadows, with a lamp.*

TILLY: Nice one Bea.

BEA:            (*Lew Ayres Voice*)  'We fight.  We try not to
                be killed, but sometimes we are – that's all'.

TILLY:          All Quiet on the Western Front?

BEA:            (*Own voice*)  Hope so.

### Boom (instrumental)

*Slow, with tinkling jazz piano.*

## SCENE SEVENTEEN:   Embassy Ball Rooms, Welling – 11th December 1936

*There is a large dance area, some tables and a small stage.  A quiet musical rendition of Brick by Brick plays in the background.  People are eagerly awaiting the arrival of the singing star GLORIA DUVALL.  Her agent TRUSTY is swallowing gallons of drink, surrounded by REPORTERS.*

REPORTERS:      When can we expect to hear Miss Duvall's latest number?

Has Miss Duvall been offered airtime on the BBC television service?

Is she really a friend of Wallace Simpson?

Did she actually visit Eaton in the summer of last year?

What did she think of the Prime Minister?

Does she really cook all her own meals?

Is there any truth in the rumour that Miss Duvall is dating a well know footballer?

TRUSTY:         I'm her agent, not her nanny.

TILLY:          (*To Howard*)   She is actually coming?

HOWARD:         Of course she's coming, I've sent a car for her from Williams.

TILLY:          You paid for a hire car?

HOWARD:         This is a top rate personality we're talking about, you can't ask her to bundle into a sidecar.

TILLY:          Well I think it's a ridiculous waste of money.

HOWARD:         She is 'the money' Till.  Look at how many people are here, just to see her sing.

TILLY:          I hope she's worth it.

HOWARD: As long as they stop here and keep drinking, she will be.

LUCY: Is she coming Till?

TILLY: We'll see darling, we'll see.

HOWARD: No sign of Shanks and his cronies?

TILLY: Maybe they found something better to do?

HOWARD: I told Mickey to keep an eye out, but they never showed up for their money.

*HURST and ALICE enter, she is guides him to a seat.*

HOWARD: Mr. Hurst, so glad you could make it.

HURST: I got sheep to tend to.

ALICE: Come and sit down, that's it. I'll get you a drink.

HURST: I ain't got time for barn dances, there's cow's to milk up at the farm.

ALICE: Sit there, I won't be a moment.

*The Vickers' girls are sitting in another part of the dance hall.*

BEA: Do you think that agent would be interested in me?

IRIS: Not unless you've got a bottle of whisky up your sleeve.

TILLY: What's that?

IRIS: Bea's trying to poach Gloria Duvall's agent.

LUCY: She seems a bit drunk.

MAY: Good, we'll get her to sign us all up.

| | |
|---|---|
| TILLY: | She spotted Duvall at a talent contest four years ago. |
| GINNY: | Blimey the competition must have been rough. |
| BEA: | Oh be fair. You have to admit she's got a great voice. |
| MAY: | No better than any of us. |
| TILLY: | Just a case of being in the right place at the right time? |
| LUCY: | Hey look, here's Katherine. |
| TILLY: | Katharine! You managed to get away then? |
| KATHERINE: | I thought he'd never leave. |
| IRIS: | Tonight's the night? |
| KATHERINE: | Yes, I've packed all my things - got my money tin ready - and the boat leaves from Erith at midnight. |
| TILLY: | And he's got no idea? |
| KATHERINE: | None. |
| LUCY: | Will you send us a post card? |
| TILLY: | Make it a letter, we don't want the old girl seeing the picture and sending him after you. |
| KATHERINE: | Have I missed Miss Duvall? |
| MAY: | You'll be lucky to see her at all, if you're going at midnight. |

*MR. TENCH enters, he looks around and sees HURST.*

| | |
|---|---|
| TENCH: | Mr. Hurst? Do you remember me? |
| HURST: | Are you the carter? |
| TENCH: | No sir. The name's Tench, you knew my father. |

HURST:          Tench, Tench?  Builder?

TENCH:          That's right.

HURST:          Get away from me, you parasite!  I'm not
                selling, you hear, never!

*ALICE rushes over.*

ALICE:          It's all right, it's all right.  (*Then to Tench*)
                What do you want?  We haven't got anything
                left.

TENCH:          I realise that Miss Hurst...

ALICE:          Then you'd best be on your way.

TENCH:          I've got something for your father.  Here,
                perhaps you should give it to him?

ALICE:          What is it?

TENCH:          It's a cheque.  Your sisters asked me to give
                him half of the sale price on the old farm.
                There's some money on top of that from the
                sale of the houses too; it's a very pleasant
                estate.

ALICE:          I...  I don't know what to say.

TENCH:          We aren't all villains Miss Hurst:  people need
                to be housed.

ALICE:          Do you expect me to thank you?

TENCH:          No.  No I don't miss.

*TENCH tips his hat and exits, passing GLORIA
DUVALL on her way in.*

RUTH:           She's here!

*The band strikes up a fanfare as GLORIA glides across
the room and up onto the stage.  The crowd cheers and*

*claps and she soaks in the admiration.  HOWARD
leaps onto the stage.*

HOWARD:        Ladies and gentlemen, I'd like to thank you all
for coming to the opening night here at the
Embassy Ballrooms.  Without further ado let
me introduce the star of the evening:  Miss
Gloria Duvall.

*The band play the intro to her most popular number and
GLORIA steps up to the microphone.  She opens her
mouth to sing as...*

*DOT staggers in, carrying a large wireless.*

DOT:        Everyone listen!  Listen to this!

*The music peters out, much to GLORIA's annoyance, as
DOT turns up the volume.*

BEA:        What is it?

DOT:        The King.

EDWARD VIII (V.O.):  ...After long and anxious consideration
I have determined to renounce the throne to
which I succeeded on the death of my father
and I am now communicating this, my final
and irrevocable decision.  I want you to
understand that in making up my mind I did
not forget the country or the Empire, which as
Prince of Wales, and lately as King, I have for
twenty-five years tried to serve.  But you must
believe me when I tell you that I have found it
impossible to discharge my duties as King, as I
would wish to do, without the help and support
of the woman I love.  The decision is mine
alone.  The other person most concerned has
tried to persuade me to take a different course.
God bless you all.  God save the King.

*A stunned silence fills the room.
All of a sudden the REPORTERS burst into life and fall
over each other scrambling out of the door.*

BEA:        He's actually done it?

ISOBEL:    Love is greater than duty.

SARAH:     Love? Love? He's got responsibilities.

RUTH:      Well, if this is the way they carry on then the
           sooner we're rid of them the better.

MAY:       How can you say that?

MARY:      Thank gawd we've kicked them all out from
           'round here I say.

HOWARD:    This is the King we're talking about.

HURST:     The King's dead? We only just buried his
           father.

ALICE:     Not dead pa, abdicated.

TILLY:     I bet Adolf's rubbing his hands.

LUCY:      Is there going to be a war now Till?

MAY:       Perhaps that old gypsy was right?

JANE:      We have still got a King you know? Albert'll
           take over, that's all.

MARY:      Bertie? I met him, when he came down to
           Crayford to re-open the Princesses Theatre.

ISOBEL:    Oh yeah. I suppose they're like trolley busses:
           all waiting at the depot.

RUTH:      King Bertie?

ISOBEL:    She should keep her hands off him, that
           American cow.

GLORIA:    (*In a sickly voice*) Well, I'm not about to be
           upstaged by a box of wires!

*GLORIA turns and steps off the stage.*

HOWARD:    Wait! Miss Duvall, wait!

TILLY: Can you believe that?

IRIS: Well, he did interrupt her song.

BEA: She's far to nasal.

TILLY: (*Shouting across to Trusty*)  I hope we'll get a refund for this?

TRUSTY: Look, I'm sorry OK?   But talent is hard to find.  You just have to put up with what comes with it.

RUTH: Come on Iso, let's go home.

TILLY: No, it's alright everyone, there's still the main attraction.

ISOBEL: Main attraction?

TRUSTY: What main attraction?

JANE: (*To Mary*)  They'll have a job following that.

TILLY: (*To Trusty*)  Are you going to get her back here or what?

TRUSTY: Like I said, I'm not her nanny.  If I could find talent <u>and</u> reliability I'd drop her tomorrow, 'til then I'll make do with fifty percent of the deal.

*BOMULLOCK enters, holding KATHERINE's money tin.*

BOMULLOCK: Where is she!!

JANE: Do you think this is the 'main attraction'?

*He shouts to her from across the room.*

BOMULLOCK: Thought you'd slip one over on me did you? Make a fool out of me in front of your new friends?

KATHERINE: He's got my money.

BOMULLOCK: Saving up for a rainy day where you? While I worked my fingers to the bone?

IRIS: Leave her alone.

BOMULLOCK: You get back where you belong, right now!

KATHERINE: No.

BOMULLOCK: What!

KATHERINE: You heard me. I said, no.

*There are slight smiles of admiration all around. BOMULLOCK narrows his eyes and then, without warning, strikes KATHERINE across the face with the tin – sending coins cascading across the floor. He grabs her by the hair and starts to drag her out. Suddenly the HOODED FIGURE appears at the doorway.*

FIGURE: Let her go!

*HURST screams.*

HURST: He's come for me! He's come for me!!!

*EVERYONE screams.*
*Pause, as BOMULLOCK decides what to do.*

FIGURE: I said, let her go.

BOMULLOCK: Who are you?

FIGURE: You know me alright.

BOMULLOCK: Show yourself.

FIGURE: Have you forgotten me so soon?

*Beat.*

BOMULLOCK: (*Nervously*) Jack?

*BOMULLOCK releases KATHERINE. The FIGURE*
*steps into the light and we see he has a white half faced*
*mask.*

FIGURE:       Thought you'd seen the last of me?

BOMULLOCK:  Wh... what's happened to your face?

FIGURE:       My plane burst into flames, as it hit the ground.

BOMULLOCK:  Then you're...?

*BOMULLOCK nervously reaches out to touch him and*
*is surprised that the figure is flesh and blood.*

BOMULLOCK:  Alive?

HURST:       Alive!?

FIGURE:       Oh, I'm alive alright.

*The FIGURE punches BOMULLOCK in the face,*
*knocking him to the floor.*

FIGURE:       And I've seen the way you've been treating
              her.  Now, go pack your things and get out of
              my house.

BOMULLOCK:  Your house?

FIGURE:       You bought it with my money didn't you?
              Forged my name on the deeds?

*BOMULLOCK cowers away.*

FIGURE:       Then I suggest you do as I say, unless you
              want to stick around for the Coppers?

BOMULLOCK:  But where will I go Jack?

FIGURE:       I don't care where you go.  Just make sure you
              never, ever, come anywhere near my wife
              again.

*BOMULLOCK grits his teeth, knowing he is defeated.*
*An excited MOTHER BOMULLOCK rushes in.*

M BOMULLOCK: (*Elated*) He's alive! It was him! Jack's alive and he's coming to...

*BOMULLOCK exits sorrowfully past his mother.*

M BOMULLOCK: (*Her enthusiasm peters out*)...make amends...

*HOWARD returns, without GLORIA.*

KATHERINE: (*To the Figure*) Why didn't you let me know? All this time?

FIGURE: After I came out of hospital, here at Frognal, I came to see you. But by then he'd moved in and, as you seemed happy, I decided it would be better if I didn't return. So I came back here. There were so many empty old houses it was easy to keep out of sight; forests, acres of farmland to get lost in. But, as the building increased, it became harder to find places to hide. Then I saw you, in what used to be the old West Wood lane. I couldn't believe it at first, so I followed you to the house. I wanted one last look, before I followed the Jarrow men back, to disappear up North. Then I saw how he treated you; how you weren't happy at all, and I could have died. He hasn't changed since we were kids, he's always been a bully. I thought maybe the war had softened him, made him see another side to life, but no. And to think I'd left you to that.

KATHERINE: But you're here now.

FIGURE: I'm not the same person I was Katherine. I've changed beyond all recognition. I asked them not to tell you I was alive, but they wouldn't give me a false death certificate. That's why my money still comes through, as far as they knew I'd gone home.

KATHERINE: Why didn't you come home?

FIGURE: The doctors at Frognal did their best, but you can't repair nature with man made tools.

KATHERINE:  Do you think I care what you look like?

FIGURE:  Even if I look like this?

*With his back to the audience the FIGURE removes his mask and holds it high in the air. There is a gasp of horror from the people who now witness his disfigured face. KATHERINE too is slightly taken aback, but only for a moment. She steps forward and kisses him passionately.*

KATHERINE:  Let's go home Jack.

*JACK throws the mask to the floor and the two of them exit, arm in arm.*
*Silence.*

HURST:  So he wasn't here for me then?

*There is a sigh of relief from everyone, as they relax.*

BEA:  'Always the same. People come. People go. Nothing ever happens'.

TILLY:  Lewis Stone, Grand Hotel.

IRIS:  One day you'll find a use for that talent.

TILLY:  Just a minute: 'The ghost of the last war'.

BEA:  What?

TILLY:  The fortune teller said: 'The ghost of the last war, will return to haunt us once more'.

LUCY:  And 'flames from the sky'?

TILLY:  It's Jack. They thought he'd died in the plane crash: He's the ghost of the Great War, back from the dead – the Manor House Ghost.

IRIS:  So?

TILLY:  So that means that the Teller's prediction has come true.

BEA:            Yes.

TILLY:         Which means there's not going to be another war. Perhaps this is a fresh start – for all of us?

IRIS:            Right.

TILLY:         So if that doesn't give us a cause to celebrate, I don't know what does?

HOWARD:     Except now we don't have a star.

TILLY:         We haven't got a king either, but I don't see the sky falling in. We'll have another one tomorrow.

BEA:            Who says we can't all be stars?

TILLY:         That's right, who says?

*MUSIC for 'Brick by Brick' tumbles into action. The following is sung over the main tune, with a different melody. The dance hall explodes into a frenzy of enjoyment and relief as...*

### Boom, Boom, Boom

All:           Boom, boom, boom,
Boom, boom, boom,
Boom, boom, boom,

Come on and dance the night away,
While the band, close at hand, begin to play
If you're town or country that's OK,
Come on, step up and be entertained.

Step by step,
Step by step,
Step by step.

Forget your worries, forget your cares,
Let that thumping rhythm take you unawares,
All you square cats get up off your chairs,
Use that talent, it's a good time premier.

Darren Rapier

Step by step,
Step by step,
Step by step.

Hear those drums beat boom, boom, boom,
The sound turns around and ripples round the
room,
It's a jump jive soul revive good time
honeymoon,
Let your heart go boom, boom, boom, boom!

Boom, boom, boom,
Boom, boom, boom,
Boom, boom, boom.

*Music break.*
*Then with audience*:

Boom, boom, boom,
Boom, boom, boom,
Boom, boom, boom.

*Music flourishes.*

Step by step,
Boom, boom, boom,
Brick by brick.

*Music flourishes to crescendo.*

Boom!


**CURTAIN**


© Darren Rapier 14th March 2000 and 12th September 2008

Other Plays by the same author include:


THE THIEFTAKER

PEOPLE IN GLASS HOUSES

SMOKE

BOOM

EXTENSIONS OF LOVE

THE SNOW QUEEN

WORLDS APART

1001 ARABIAN NIGHTS

CLARA AND THE NUTCRACKER


www.darrenrapier.co.uk

## DARREN RAPIER

Darren Rapier trained at Rose Bruford College, graduating in 1995 with a degree in writing. He has written for film, television and theatre. Plays include *The Thieftaker,* about the first real gangster in early Eighteenth Century London; *People in Glass Houses*, a futuristic absurd comedy; *Smoke*, a play with music, about the railway 'improvements' and clearances of 1863; *Boom*, a community play set in 1936, about the housing boom in the South East; *Extensions of Love*, about one woman's obsession with another and *Worlds Apart*, set in India and the UK. Adaptations for children have included *The Snow Queen, The Little Mermaid, 1001 Arabian Nights* and *Clara and the Nutcracker.* Short plays include *The Gallery,* and the ten minute musical *Dying for a Kipp* at Greenwich Theatre. In 2007 he wrote and co-directed *Payback* for Greenwich and Lewisham Young Peoples' Theatre and *Departures* for the National Youth Theatre. He has written and directed two short films *It Is* and *The Race,* is a writer on *Doctors* for the BBC and has two feature films in development. Darren has been short listed for the Carl Forman Award at BAFTA, is a selected short film writer for TAPS and was a finalists in the BBC Talent Television Drama initiative in 2002. His radio play *Vital Statistics* was part of BBC Radio Drama/Hampstead Theatre's 'Stages of Sound' 2006. Darren is also Artistic Director of *Spanner in the Works,* who run drama based workshops in schools, hospitals and museums and a freelance drama trainer and facilitator.

www.ingramcontent.com/pod-product-compliance
Lightning Source LLC
Chambersburg PA
CBHW060424260626
47161CB00005B/1780